Steel Wombs

R. C. LINDHOLM

Copyright © 2017 R. C. Lindholm.

All rights reserved. No part of this book may be reproduced, stored, or transmitted by any means—whether auditory, graphic, mechanical, or electronic—without written permission of the author, except in the case of brief excerpts used in critical articles and reviews. Unauthorized reproduction of any part of this work is illegal and is punishable by law.

Steel Wombs is a work of fiction. Names, characters, and incidents are the product of the author's imagination or are used fictitiously. Any resemblance to actual events, locals, or persons, living or dead, is entirely coincidental.

ISBN: 978-1-4834-6624-8 (sc)
ISBN: 978-1-4834-6626-2 (hc)
ISBN: 978-1-4834-6625-5 (e)

Library of Congress Control Number: 2017902852

Because of the dynamic nature of the Internet, any web addresses or links contained in this book may have changed since publication and may no longer be valid. The views expressed in this work are solely those of the author and do not necessarily reflect the views of the publisher, and the publisher hereby disclaims any responsibility for them.

Any people depicted in stock imagery provided by Thinkstock are models, and such images are being used for illustrative purposes only.
Certain stock imagery © Thinkstock.

Lulu Publishing Services rev. date: 03/09/2017

This book is for my wife, Betty, the love of my life. If not for her support and prodding, it would never have seen the light of day.

Contents

Chapter 1	Hounds of the Backer Villen	1
Chapter 2	A Call from Kristianstad	3
Chapter 3	Rescue above Djúpalónssandur Beach	8
Chapter 4	Absolut Meeting	13
Chapter 5	Wounded Thumb	27
Chapter 6	Vasteras Cousins	35
Chapter 7	Hermit Crab Comes out of Her Shell	39
Chapter 8	A Room in Siena	52
Chapter 9	Morning Fog and Two Etruscan Lovers	60
Chapter 10	A Mysterious Island	72
Chapter 11	A Lilliputian Fence	82
Chapter 12	The Lab	88
Chapter 13	A Note on the Floor	96
Chapter 14	Hello, Kara O'Malley	106
Chapter 15	Call for Help	116
Chapter 16	All Drowned	124
Chapter 17	Home to Sweden	140
Chapter 18	Great Blasket	143
Chapter 19	Good-Bye, My Love	156

Acknowledgments 161
About the Author 163

Chapter 1

Hounds of the Backer Villen

Lech realized he was being dragged through the hall by his feet, a trail of blood and water staining the cold marble floor. The heavy steel door creaked open, and she grabbed him under the arms and tossed him like a rag doll onto the gravel path.

Lech's head hit the gravel first, and wooziness soon pinned him to the ground. As his vision cleared, he regretted testing his theory that women found him irresistible. He tried to remember why he'd ever left Poland to join this German research facility in Backer Villen.

The order had been simple enough: deliver a packet of requisition forms for the fräulein's signature. When he arrived, her apartment door stood open. He'd heard there was a hot tub in the middle of her living room, but he never expected to see her bathing in it. He cleared his throat and waited. She sat with her back to him. Snapping her fingers, she motioned for him to come in.

"Fräulein, I have some papers for you."

"Put them on the desk." Her icy tone should have been warning enough.

After laying the papers in a neat pile on the otherwise empty desk, he dared to approach the tub.

"Fräulein, you are magnificent."

"So! Is that why you stand, gawking at me, Herr Wojcik?"

"Yes. I am a great admirer of beauty." He stooped, allowing his hands to explore her breasts before continuing across the tight belly. Fast as a cobra, she grabbed him by the back of the neck and pulled him facedown into the steaming water. He struggled but couldn't break her grip and began to choke.

"Is the view better?" she asked.

When he'd nearly passed out, she rose, lifted, and shoved him toward her desk. He stumbled across the room and fell, hitting his head on the lion-claw leg.

He lay on the gravel and rolled over to see her still naked, hovering over him. The magnitude of his mistake crystallized when he looked down the path. Her feral laugh was now mingled with the familiar sound of large dogs running on gravel. He loved dogs, but these were different. They never responded to a friendly scratch on the head, and their eyes were empty, devoid of feeling. Apollo, the huge German shepherd, reached Lech first and sank his teeth into an outstretched arm. The other dogs followed and tore into the body. The pain ended as blood soaked the gravel path.

When it was over and the dogs quieted, she patted Apollo's blood-covered snout. "You did an excellent job, my little ones. Now we must get you cleaned up."

Chapter 2

A Call from Kristianstad

Cal Larsson tossed books into two cardboard boxes, one labeled *Home* and the other *Library*. Some were headed to his home office, the rest to the geology library at Sanford College in North Carolina, where he'd taught for thirty years. *Dana's Textbook on Mineralogy* landed in the home box, even though it was already too heavy. "Damn! I've got to put more of these books in the library box," he said.

"Talking to yourself?" Dan Morris stepped over an already-filled box that blocked the path into the office. They had been friends since they shared a basement office as untenured instructors.

"This is worse than I thought," Cal said. "What to keep? What to dump? I have to get this place cleaned out."

"You can keep the office, you know. With emeritus status comes a desk, chair, and cup of coffee."

"No. I'm not sure what I'll be doing, but it won't be here."

"Are all those going too?" Dan asked, waving toward steel shelves sagging under neatly labeled rock samples. "Still claiming they're material for future research?"

"Don't think so, but I can make one hell of a stone wall."

"Good deal, and I could use it for geology field trips."

"Take anything you want," Cal said, "including books, but remember my strict no-return policy."

Within minutes, Dan had filled two boxes.

"Aren't you afraid Linda will have your scalp when you bring home more books?" Cal asked.

"Not a problem, my friend; I'll sneak them into the garage and conduct a relocation program while she's at work."

"You are a devious person, Dan."

"You could learn these little tricks if you'd do yourself a favor and find a female."

"Any candidates?"

"How about the one on your desk?"

Cal reached over and picked up a photograph of a young woman pointing to a rock outcrop and wearing a playful smile. "Kara O'Malley?"

"Yes. As I recall, you two were a hot item for years."

"We were. White hot. Came close to tying the knot when we worked together in the Shell lab in Houston. Things were good, but then I decided to come here. I think she half blamed you because you recommended me for the job."

"I never did understand that. She liked the States and could have stayed here."

"True, but then her friend Pat Narey started an environmental geology company in Galway and begged her to take over. The opportunity to run a small business and go back in Ireland was irresistible. In the end, career trumped love."

"So that was that?"

Cal shrugged and looked at Kara's picture. Vacations together, phone calls, e-mails—all stopped. *Guess distance doesn't make the heart grow fonder after all*, he thought, caressing the frame holding the small photo. "When do you plan to do the dirty deed, Dan?"

"Which dirty deed? I have a lot of them on my bucket list."

"Retirement."

"A couple more years. I'm still trying to figure it out." Dan reached over and picked up the one remaining photograph from Cal's desk. "You aren't going to leave *this*, are you?"

"No. That's the only one of my brother-in-law." As Cal said this, the memory of the oil field accident that had killed Ben flashed across his mind.

Dan put his hand on Cal's shoulder. "Thinking about West Texas?"

"Yeah. They'd only been married five years when it happened."

"I remember the wedding. They were a perfect couple. How is she these days?"

"Super! Got tired of being a secretary and went back to school. You knew she was going to UNC, didn't you?"

"I did. Is she finished?"

"In a month—and that's a graduation I won't miss."

Dan started to fill another box with scavenged books. As Cal held Kara's photograph, he remembered the young women he'd taught at Sanford. But he still missed her. He closed his eyes and put the photograph carefully on the top of the books for his home office. "Say, Dan, how about lunch?"

"Okay. Carolina Grill?"

Cal nodded. "Where else?"

As they were leaving, the phone rang. "Damn! Let's go. If it's important, they'll call again," Cal said.

"Answer it. I'll get a table."

The caller ID display showed *Kristianstad, Sweden—Mark Svendson*. "What could Mark be calling about? Haven't seen him for an age," Cal told the empty office.

"Cal, this is Mark Svendson. How are you?"

"Fine, and you?"

"Terrific, pal. Are you up for a trip to Sweden?"

"I'm visiting Swedish cousins in Vasteras next week. Why?"

"I have a friend looking for advice from a scientist who knows something about biology and might be available for several weeks, and if I remember, you had a biology minor. When I mentioned you, she said she met you once and you'd be perfect. Would you be willing to meet with her?"

"What's her name?"

"Sorry, pal, she said not over the phone or Internet."

"She sounds like that famous mystery, wrapped in an enigma."

"That pretty well sums it up. She's single, drop-dead gorgeous, and nearly as old as you, so you won't feel like you're robbing the cradle. When would you be here?"

"I already have my tickets, but I can change them and see your friend before Vasteras. I'll e-mail once I sort out the tickets."

"She'll be pleased. Have a good trip. See you soon."

Cal hung up, hoping the mysterious, drop-dead-gorgeous woman might save him from the funk he'd been in since receiving his AARP card. He turned to his desk and stared at photographs of Kara and Ben. He remembered how hard it had been to convince Brenda and her daughters to move to North Carolina after Ben's death. For twenty years, Cindy and Sara were more like his daughters than nieces. Cal knew that nothing stayed the same forever and that Brenda and her family wouldn't always live as close as they did now. Retirement put this in perspective, and he was beginning to dread life as a lonely old man. He picked up Kara's photograph again. *Damn, we were a great match*, he mused, *or so I thought. How could we have been so stupid to give each other up? I guess by now you're married, not searching for a secondhand geologist.* He put the photographs in his briefcase and headed for the Carolina Grill.

Cal secured his seat belt and got comfortable, ready for some light reading. His iPad had two Longmire mysteries. He hated long, unbroken transatlantic flights, so his travel plans always included a break to visit someplace where he could take some good pictures. On this trip, it would be a tour of the Snæfellsnes Peninsula, north of Reykjavik.

A voice on the intercom announced they would be on the ground in twenty minutes. Cal prepared himself for the landing. He hated this part of flying and concentrated on the ocean below, hoping to find something that would take his mind off the runway ahead. He could see Iceland's coast and Reykjavik beyond it. After he dropped his bags at the hotel, he wandered around the docks experimenting with his new digital camera, which took superb photos and fit into his shirt pocket.

Early the next morning, he joined five other passengers in a Chevy van for a daylong tour. His traveling companions were two elderly couples from Virginia Beach and a strawberry blonde from California. She took the seat next to the driver. *Win some, lose some*, Cal thought, sitting alone in the back with his camera.

The van stopped, and everyone walked down a steep trail to Djúpalónssandur Beach. This unique section of the shore was paved with rounded jet-black pebbles alleged to possess magical properties. Cal dropped several small ones into his pocket. *Never know when a little magic might come in handy*, he thought, trying to picture the gorgeous Swede he would soon meet.

Back in the van, Cal examined the shiny black pebbles and hoped no one saw him take them. He felt guilty because this was a national park, and taking souvenirs, even small, magical ones, was strictly forbidden. He rationalized his bad behavior by promising to give Dan some for his class on the way sedimentary environments control pebble shape.

The driver pointed out Arnarstapi's scenic harbor, filled with colorful boats returned from deep offshore fishing. Cal settled in for the return trip to Reykjavik. So far, he was enjoying the break in the flight from Dulles to Copenhagen but regretted there was no one to share it. Cal put his hand in his pocket and touched the pebble. He could still change his ticket to include a stop in Ireland. Maybe he could try the magic pebbles on Kara O'Malley.

Chapter 3

Rescue above Djúpalónssandur Beach

Cal shielded his eyes against the bright sun and gazed at the ragged cliffs of black basalt rising straight out of the pounding surf. In the distance, spires of rock emerged from the ocean like ancient sentinels protecting Iceland from Atlantic storms. Cal loved this place but wished he could pronounce its name.

"Somebody's in trouble!" the girl from California shouted. Cal turned and saw a woman with long black hair running toward them.

She called, "Oh, please help us! Kathleen fell! She'll die!"

Cal got out of the van and followed her to the edge of the basalt cliff. He looked over at the waves that beat on the rock, filling the air with a chilly mist. Ten feet below them, a young girl huddled on a narrow ledge. Eleven or twelve, Cal guessed, and a miniature of her mother.

A husky man with his right arm in a sling stood at the cliff's edge. When he saw Cal, he extended his good hand. "Dear God, help her! I'd be going down, but for this damned arm. Mary says I'd kill us both."

All the other members of the tour crowded around Cal. "I have an idea," he said, but before he could finish, the tour leader ran up, waving nylon rope. "Hold on! Put this on. I did the best I could to make a harness. Crude, but it should work."

"Thanks. A lot better than going down with no safety lines."

"Here's another piece of rope for the girl."

Cal took it and hollered, "I'm coming down now, so don't move, Kathleen, okay?"

"Not an inch." Her answer was nearly lost in the noise of the waves crashing below.

"Good girl, not an inch." He put on the makeshift harness and eased down onto the cliff face. It was immediately clear it was going to be tricky. There were more fractures in the basalt than he'd seen from the top. His first handhold threatened to dislodge an enormous rock. *If that falls, she's gone, and me with her*, he thought. He leaned out for a better view of the rock face while working his way down as fast as he dared. When he reached her ledge, he bent down and squeezed the girl's shoulder. "How are you doing?"

She nodded.

"You'll be fine. I'm going to tie this rope around your waist. Hang on to it, and they'll pull you up. Use your feet to push away from the rock." He knotted the rope, tugged to test it, and waved to the group transfixed by the drama below them. He held his breath as she rose up the cliff to her parents' waiting arms. As he began his own climb, the ledge broke; he slid down the rough face. He winced as the serrated rock sliced into his legs before the safety line stopped his fall with a jolt, leaving him hanging in midair. He froze; his heart pounded until he was able to draw a deep breath. "Keep the line taut," he called. "Don't try to pull me up; just let me climb." He stretched to put his hand into a large crevice and pulled until his foot touched a solid ledge, continuing until several hands grabbed him.

He collapsed onto the grass as the realization of just how lucky they had been swept over him. Kathleen's father pulled him up and wrapped him in a one-armed embrace. "I'm Sean O'Sullivan. I can never repay you for what you did." He beamed as his wife began to sing an Irish blessing. "May the wind always be at your back, and may the sun shine warm on your face."

Kathleen stood by her mother and grinned at Cal. He wondered, was she embarrassed by the fuss she'd caused, or now that it was over, had she enjoyed the adventure?

He knelt next to her. "You're a lucky girl to have parents who love you so much."

"I know. What you did was brave."

"My Gaelic mountain goat, you were pretty courageous yourself. Very cool. No panic." He brushed aside her ebony bangs. "How did you get yourself into that fix anyway?"

Kathleen opened a small bag hanging around her neck and pulled out a glistening white crystal. "Zeolite. The one called chabazite, I think."

Cal took the crystal from her bruised hand. "It is," he said and smiled. "I'm a geologist, so I can almost understand why you'd make a dangerous climb like that to collect crystals. But take it from me—pretty as they are, they're not worth the risk."

She reached out and put one in his hand. "Would you like one?"

"Sure." He admired the white crystal, dropped it into his shirt pocket. "Thanks. I'll think of you whenever I look at it."

Sean O'Sullivan reached out and stroked Kathleen's jet-black hair. "She wants to be a mineralogist. I'm not sure whether this will cure her or make her more determined."

"More determined, I'd bet."

"Yes." She laughed. "More determined."

She pointed to the deep cuts on Cal's legs, visible under his shredded pants leg. "You're hurt."

"I'll live." Then he noticed her legs were also covered with scratches. "They probably hurt too."

"They sting a bit. I was only a few feet down when a rock broke. I slid till the ledge caught me. I really thought I was going to die. Then you came down. I'll never forget your face. Never!"

"Nor I yours," Cal said.

"Time to go, Kathleen." Her father took her arm and pulled her up. "Cal Larsson, come to Killybegs, and we'll give you a proper Irish thanks."

"You know, Sean, I might just do that."

The O'Sullivans waved and walked toward the beach. Then Cal noticed his pants pocket had ripped open when he slid down the jagged rock face. The magic pebbles from Djúpalónssandur Beach were gone, but now at least he had Kathleen's crystal.

He sat down on the grass again, trying to forget how this day might have had a different ending.

"That could use a little TLC." The girl from California sat beside him. "I'm a nurse, and I brought a few tools of the trade." Digging into her rucksack, she pulled out a first aid kit. "I heard your name is Cal. Mine is Sally Davis. I'm from San Diego."

She radiates the suntanned appeal a young woman from San Diego would have, he thought.

After tearing a bigger hole in his pants, she cleaned the deepest wound and covered it with a large bandage. "That should take care of you."

"I'm glad you came prepared."

"Girl Scout training." She smiled.

"What brings you to Iceland, aside from patching up injured geologists?"

"I'm meeting my boyfriend tomorrow, and we're driving along the south coast from Reykjavik to the Vatnajökull Glacier."

"You'll see the big glacier while it still has ice."

"It's melting, isn't it?"

"Three feet a year. In a century, it may be all gone."

"Another casualty of global warming?"

"It is."

"What about the dolts who say the whole thing's a hoax?"

"Guess they've never visited a glacier." Cal laughed.

The van driver began rounding up his passengers to begin their return trip. Cal and his new seatmate spent the rest of the trip talking about everything from climate change to California politics to collecting zeolites. The tour left him wishing he was driving around Iceland with a pretty girl from Ireland.

The next morning, Cal caught the airport shuttle and soon was on his way to Copenhagen. He took the first train to Kristianstad, in southern Sweden, where he looked forward to seeing Mark Svendson and meeting his mysterious friend.

Fifteen hundred miles away, a phone rang near the main arena for the Greater Berlin Dog Show. A woman pulled out her cell phone.

"Must we talk right now? You need to trust me, Adolph. I was with her from the moment she got back to Sweden. Nothing happened. Just went to the university and visited her family."

Before he could finish, she interrupted. "Yes, yes. I'm going back this afternoon, as soon as the show ends."

Massaging her short white hair, she glanced toward the center ring where owners gathered with their dogs. "Must I remind you, I also was trained by Uncle Markus? I know my job and won't do anything to threaten our work. Don't bother me anymore. I have to get Apollo now." She slammed the phone to the ground.

Chapter 4

Absolut Meeting

As the train pulled into the station, Cal saw Mark waiting on the platform. He gathered his bags and rushed out to meet his friend, remembering Swedish trains wait for no man.

"Hi, Cal! Welcome to Kristianstad! Been a long time."

"Far too long."

"It has been. Grab your bags, and let's go. My car is parked over there," Mark said, pointing to a cherry-red Saab.

Cal slipped into front seat and whistled. "Pretty nice. These 9-3 Aero sedans don't come cheap. Life must be good."

"Very good indeed. A few years ago, I hooked up with a Norwegian petroleum company working in the North Sea. Mostly involves maps, something I can do in my office here in Kristianstad."

"No trips to the oil platforms?" Cal asked.

"God no! Never been to one. I go to Stavanger every few months. Flights to Oslo don't take long, so it's not bad. You should come over and give it a try."

"I haven't gotten used to the idea of retirement yet, but might be interested in some low-stress consulting. I'll be in Stockholm in a week or so. Maybe you could give me several leads."

"Consider it done. How are Brenda and the girls?"

"Fine. And your family?"

"Liv works for a company, making the best geologic maps in Europe. A few months ago, she became assistant to the CEO. Jim is studying at Uppsala. Followed his old man into geology."

"You must be proud."

"You know it. Say, Cal, what about your cute little Irish friend?"

"Do you mean Kara O'Malley?"

"Yes, or are you involved with more than one cute little Irish friend?"

"Funny you should ask. I did meet another one yesterday, but she's only eleven. Actually, I haven't seen Kara recently, but not by choice."

"Good Lord, you're still carrying that torch? Didn't the bloody thing burn out a long time ago?"

"The flame is low, but not completely out. We used to talk on the phone and exchange e-mails. Now, nothing but silence. I don't I understand what happened. I've worked hard to forget her, but can't seem to do it."

"Not to probe, but does she love you?"

"She did once, but careers, distance, religion all got in the way. Now I'm not so sure."

"In case you don't have a mirror, my friend, your gray beard isn't getting any darker. I hope I got to you in time. I'll bet Inga can solve your problem. She's smart, bright, and blonde. As a matter of fact, you met her thirty years ago."

"Did I? Where?"

"In Moscow, at the International Geological Congress in '84."

"You never said she's a geologist."

"She's not, but a group of immunologists were meeting there at the same time. She was still a student and had lunch with us. To tell you the truth, I was sweet on her at the time."

"What did your wife think about you and Inga?"

"Oh, I hadn't met Liv yet. Inga and I go back to high school days. Just couldn't get anywhere with her, not like I didn't try. Right away, she took a shine to you. Never understood that."

"Could be she's a woman with excellent taste? Come on, Mark, help me out. Inga still doesn't register."

"Think about a tall, willowy, twenty-year-old platinum blonde. She has a slight limp because of a riding accident when she was a kid, but it's never slowed her down."

"How could I have forgotten? She was stunning. Isn't her name Rund-something?"

"Still is stunning, and the name is Rundstrom."

"And she's the one with some nameless problem? But why me?"

"She remembers you from Moscow and wants help from someone she can trust. When I mentioned that you had a minor in biology that seemed to cinch it. Plus, you're single and retired with time to spare."

"So when do I meet her?"

"She'll be at the Absolut factory in Åhus at six o'clock. First we'll drop your bag at the hotel and get coffee."

"Okay, but why the Absolut factory? She isn't an alcoholic who's seen too many James Bond movies, is she? Seems to be pushing this secrecy thing pretty hard."

"Odd, I admit, but I guarantee she's no alcoholic. Honestly, I don't understand, but she was adamant. The last time I saw her, she seemed edgy. Almost frightened."

"Of what?"

"No clue."

"It's fine, Mark. I look forward to meeting her again." Cal pictured the pretty blonde he remembered. *Maybe she's just what I need to get past Kara.* "Let's skip coffee and head for Åhus right now."

"Sorry, pal; she said six sharp."

On the drive to Åhus, Cal's thoughts flipped between Mark's blonde Inga and the cooling embers of his love for Kara as he savored a rendezvous in the Absolut Vodka factory.

The parking lot was nearly empty. In the far corner, a black SUV was nearly hidden by an enormous sculpture of an Absolut bottle. Mark got out of the car and froze. He jumped back and stared toward the sculpture. Cal walked over to his friend and followed his stare. "What's the matter?"

"Do you remember how I feel about large dogs?"

"Scared shitless, as I recall. It was something I could never understand." Cal followed Mark's gaze to a small grove of aspens but saw nothing. "What's over there?"

"A big German shepherd, but it ran into the trees."

"Probably the owner in the SUV let it out to take a leak."

"Maybe we should wait in the car for a while."

"Aren't we supposed to meet Inga at six sharp? There's nothing out there now. Come on."

They walked to the visitors' entrance, and Mark spoke to the man sitting behind the thick plate glass window. The heavy steel door opened, and they were greeted by a young woman.

"Are you both American?" she asked in English.

"I'm not, but my friend is," Mark said.

"Welcome to Absolut. Your tour will begin shortly, so please come in and have a seat."

Ten minutes later, their escort arrived and led them up a flight of stairs to the observation deck above the production level. She explained how southern Sweden's wheat was transformed into the world's best vodka. After their escort finished, Cal had decided it was time to give Absolut a chance.

Cal walked over to Mark and shrugged. "So, where is your mysterious Inga?"

"She told me to take the tour and she'd meet us." Fifteen minutes into the tour, another eye-catching guide, dressed like a Swedish flag approached and motioned for them to follow her into a small room off the deck. She nodded and left. Cal continued into the dimly lit room, nearly colliding with a woman he immediately recognized as the secretive Inga. Mark hadn't lied. She was stunning, living up to his image from thirty years earlier.

"Dr. Cal Larsson, I'm sure you remember Dr. Inga Rundstrom."

"Nice to see you again, Dr. Rundstrom. Sorry about nearly running over you."

"The pleasure is mine." She shook his hand with the firmness of someone secure in being herself. "No need to apologize. They could use more lights in here, and please call me Inga. You did when we met in Moscow."

Mesmerized by her glacial blue eyes, he held on to her hand.

She smiled and disengaged. "Please. I may need it later."

"Sorry again." *Not off to the start I'd hoped for*, he thought.

"It's seven; is anyone hungry?" she asked. "The place on the wharf behind the factory is excellent. I adore their smoked eel." She opened the door and led them to the street.

"How did you get in without joining the tour?" Cal asked.

"My father was an associate of the president, who arranged for me to meet you as I did." She stopped and looked up and down the dark street. Mark glanced at Cal with a negative shrug.

Inga led them to a table, away from the other patrons, in the back of the restaurant. She and Mark ordered smoked eel. "I think our American visitor may want something else. Am I correct, Cal?" she asked.

"Yes. I may get brave, but fried cod and chips sound good for now."

"Outstanding choice," Mark said.

She excused herself, leaving them alone.

"Well, what do you think?"

"She's even more appealing after thirty years, and a natural blonde to boot."

Mark asked, "What makes you so sure?"

"Coloring and eyebrows all say it."

"There it is. Natural or colored? An interesting research project for you."

She returned before Cal could respond. "You boys having guy talk? Have you ordered beer yet?"

"Sorry. You didn't tell us what you wanted, so we waited," Cal said.

"I would like a Nils Oscar."

"Cal?"

"Nils Oscar for me too. When in Sweden, do as the Swedes do. Are you going to make it unanimous, Mark?"

"At the risk of seeming disloyal, I'll go with Carlsberg. I became a fan after they built a hundred-kilometer beer pipeline from the brewery in Gothenburg to the student union at Chalmers University," Mark said.

"You're kidding, right?" Cal laughed.

"I never heard such an outrageous story. A Danish joke?" She grinned.

"I don't think so. But there's more. The house Carlsberg gave to Niels Bohr came with a beer pipeline from the brewery next door."

The waitress arrived with three beers.

"Ah, beer straight from the brewery pipeline," Cal said, laughing.

She had heard part of their conversation and played along. "Yes. Straight from our own private pipeline."

Cal hoped he wasn't always so obvious, but Inga's attraction was like a strong magnet that wouldn't release his eyes. *This isn't fair*, he mused. *I have no idea what she wants me to do, but I'd be a fool to say no.*

After dinner, they all switched to Carlsberg in recognition of creative marketing and enjoyed comparing notes about the years since Moscow.

"Looks like they're trying to close up. We should be leaving, but before I forget …" Mark handed Cal an envelope. "Some people you can call in Stockholm."

"Thanks. I'll do it as soon as I get there." Cal held up the envelope and looked at Inga. "People I can talk to about possible consulting jobs."

She smiled and leaned across the table. "Your hotel is near my apartment, so come with me."

"Excellent idea. Are you okay with that, Mark?" Cal replied, daring Mark with a glance to object.

"Sure. Give me call if you need a ride tomorrow."

As he climbed into Inga's car, Cal wondered if he'd now learn about the mystery that brought him here. She pulled out of the parking lot and took the road to Kristianstad. "Tell me something about yourself," Cal said. "You seem to know a good deal about me, but I know nothing about you except we had lunch together in Moscow."

"Well, where do I start? I taught genetics and immunology at Lund for ten years. I loved the job, but when a new department opened in Kristianstad, I was offered a position as assistant chair. A difficult choice, but I would be closer to my family. They all live in this area, except for my baby sister, Louise Marie, who moved to Stockholm. Last summer, I took a year's leave of absence to work in a laboratory outside of Sweden. The job is interesting, and we are getting exceptional results, but the research bothers me. Bothers me quite a lot."

"Seems like a great job, so what could bother you?"

She raised her shoulders and gave her head a gentle shake. "Oh, it is really nothing."

"Okay, if nothing bothers you, why did you come home now?"

"Mama's eightieth birthday was last week. I wanted to be here for that. Plus, I needed time to think and desperately wanted someone else's opinion about what we are doing in the lab. From Moscow, I know you are a person I can trust."

"I'd be delighted to give you my opinion, if I had some idea what it's all about."

"Come with me to the lab," she said. "You must see for yourself."

He hesitated. *She's one puzzling woman, but I love being near her. What have I got to lose but time—and that's something I have in abundance?* "Okay, I could do that. Where is the laboratory?"

As her grip on the wheel tightened, she looked away.

"I cannot tell you that."

"Is this some sort of spook thing with the Swedish CIA?" he asked with a half smile.

"No! And nothing criminal in the strict sense." Her cagey answer was accompanied by a self-conscious laugh.

Neither spoke for a half an hour as the dark countryside rolled past. "Why is it me you're asking for help? Mark was vague. He said you wanted someone you could trust, but you must know lots of people you trust."

"I do, but it was what happened in Moscow."

Cal closed his eyes and racked his brain. Finally, he turned toward Inga and asked, "Was it about someone who died?"

"Yes. Mama had a baby much too late in life. Little Otto was never well and passed away six months before I met you. He was not a year old. I was taking care of him one night when he started to choke. Of course, I called the medical emergency number, but he was gone before help arrived."

"And you blamed yourself."

"I did, but you told me it was not my fault. Bad things sometimes happen to the best people. You said I had done the right thing. It would have happened no matter who had been there. We talked for hours. You never realized it, but you probably saved my life that night. I saw then you were a person I could trust and rely on. I nearly wrote you, but knew you wouldn't be interested is a skinny Swedish student with a limp. When I told Mark my concerns about the laboratory, he mentioned your name and hoped you might be able to help me again."

"I'll do my best, but first you've got to—" He was interrupted as they stopped in front of the hotel. He turned to face her and noticed a tear on her cheek. It was obvious he wasn't going to learn any more tonight. "Tomorrow, come by at seven, and we'll talk some more. Meet me in the lobby, and we'll get breakfast there."

"Here is another idea. I will make waffles in my apartment. I am sure mine are better than we can get here."

"Tomorrow at seven then," he said.

She flicked a sugar cube across the table in her game of table soccer, grinning as the cube skated between two wineglasses.

"One more goal for the she-wolf." Her grin turned to a sneer when she noticed that the couple at the next table looked away, avoiding eye contact. She'd been waiting impatiently for her brother to answer his phone. Finally, she heard a weary "Hello."

"Yes," she said. "Inga met the American in the vodka plant, and no, I don't understand why he's here. Maybe only wants a good lay? Who knows?" She cackled at her own joke. She listened to his response and picked another sugar cube from the bowl. "It's true. Absolut was an odd place to meet. She's a brilliant scientist; otherwise, I'd never have gotten her for the laboratory, but sometimes she's like a beautiful child. If she recognizes the car, she may realize she's being followed." The second sugar cube skated across the table and shattered on the floor. "I agree that is unlikely, but everything is under control, so don't do anything stupid."

When Cal arrived in the lobby the next morning, Inga sat with her back to the door, watching TV. He walked over and touched her shoulder. She grabbed his hand with a hard jerk and pulled him over the back of the chair. "Oh God, I am so sorry! Did I hurt you?"

He found it was hard to laugh with his feet in the air. Struggling to stand, he caught the desk clerk's bewildered expression.

"Oh, Cal, please forgive me. I cannot tell you how bad I feel. I do not understand what is wrong with me. Are you hurt?"

"Other than a bruised ego, I'm fine. Quite a move. Where did you learn it?"

"I took karate lessons for ten years and recently got my third-degree black belt."

"Next time, I'll simply say good morning." He laughed and stood, rubbing his shoulder.

"Do you still want waffles?"

"You bet. I need nourishment after my morning's karate lesson."

Inside her apartment, she went into the kitchen and brought him a steaming cup of coffee.

"Would you like cream and sugar?"

"Black is fine."

"I made the batter before I left; waffles cook quickly, so it will not be long."

He took his coffee into the dining room, which seemed familiar. The teak table was nearly identical to the one he'd given himself when he took the job at Sanford. The rest of the Scandinavian furniture was exactly what he'd have bought if it could have been found in North Carolina. In a scent cloud from Swedish waffles, Cal crossed the room to the fireplace. Several photos were lined up on the mantel. *Must be her family*, he thought.

Joining him, her arm brushed his. He found the brief touch exhilarating. "My sisters and brother. Marie Louise is on the left standing by Frederick; she is the one in Stockholm. Next are Ann Marie and Kerstin Marie. Mama is in the chair."

"Marie, Marie, Marie … did your family have an apparition of the Virgin Mary?"

"No." She smiled. "My parents never explained why they did the name thing."

"Are you Inga Marie?"

"They stopped before I was born."

She led him into the kitchen and opened the waffle iron. "That was close. Much longer and they would have been toast. Is that not an Americans saying?"

"More or less."

"I like the lingonberry, but you might prefer sugar and butter."

"I'll take all three," Cal said.

"Oink." She laughed.

There was something flirtatious in her response. He crossed the kitchen and stood next to her. "Did I hear *oink*? I distinctly heard *oink*." He lifted her chin and gave her a hard kiss, but she pulled back.

"Inga, I'm sorry. I didn't—"

She turned away. "No, it is fine. Let's eat before the waffles get cold." She handed him a plate, gesturing for him to sit.

Cal shoveled on a generous helping of butter and lingonberry jam, but no sugar. She nodded, giving him a half smile. It wasn't long until he'd cleaned the plate and reached across the table to touch her hand. "Thank you. They were delicious." He had a question about yesterday that needed an answer. "Why did we go all the way to Åhus and meet in the Absolut factory?"

"Before you arrived, I felt like I was being followed … watched. I kept seeing a black SUV. Not the most common car here. The windows were so dark, I could not look inside. I did not want them to see me with a stranger from America who might be curious about my work at the laboratory. They are very sensitive about what goes on there. Obsessed,

I would say. It seemed better to keep our meeting secret and not have it in Kristianstad."

"Why would anyone care?"

For several minutes, her fingers explored the edge of the plate. "No one, I suppose. We should forget it."

Someone does care, but why? he thought.

After breakfast, they went back into the living room and sat on the sofa. Had he misread her? As he looked around the room, he remembered a rack full of pipes next to the family photos. An old craving returned. He walked over and picked one up. "Is there tobacco to go with this?"

She joined him and cradled a beautifully carved meerschaum. "Sorry, no. It was Papa's, but he died five years ago. Do you smoke?"

"Not for twenty years. My nieces were convinced I'd be dead before they reached puberty if I didn't quit."

"Are you close to them?"

"They're like daughters to me. Their dad passed away when they were quite young. I'm the only dad they've known."

"Every girl needs a papa." She stood beside him and touched his arm. "Cal, I must make a confession."

"You're Catholic. I knew that gathering of Marias was no accident."

She ignored his joke and went into her bedroom, returning with a pile of books. "Here is what you need to read."

"Now I get it! You're Mormon. They always have books you must read."

"Please, be serious. You must learn a little immunology before you come with me to the lab."

"Let me get this straight. I'm going somewhere you can't disclose to see something you can't describe, and I must take Immunology 101? Why?"

"When we reach the lab, you will impersonate a colleague, Eric Rosander, another Swedish immunologist."

"Why didn't you ask him to go?"

"For one thing, he does not possess a grain of common sense; I've worked with him and do not trust his judgment. He would be of no help to me."

"Won't someone recognize I'm not him? And why do I have to go undercover anyway? Can't I simply be Dr. Larsson, retired geologist, traveling with a beautiful woman?"

"I am sure no one at the lab knows what he looks like. Our work is, shall we say, sensitive, and they would not be pleased with an American tourist. I am the only immunologist, so your knowledge will not need to be too convincing."

"How displeased will they be if they discover who I am?"

"I am not sure; let us hope we do not find out. First, I would undoubtedly be fired on the spot."

"Before we start, I have several things to do."

"What?"

"I'd like to go to Orrefors and buy a few presents for my sister and Swedish cousins."

"We can go today, if you want."

"That works, but one more thing. I told my cousins in Vasteras that I'd arrive on Saturday, and I need a couple of days in Stockholm."

"We cannot arrive at the lab until the twenty-sixth, so there is plenty of time. I do not think your reading will take more than a week."

"A week? Is that all?" Cal looked at the stack of material. He remembered the panic of graduate school—so much to read, so little time.

The next morning, when Cal arrived in the lobby, Inga had her back to the TV, facing the door. He laughed.

"I wanted no more sneak attacks," she said.

"Don't worry. I planned to make plenty of noise."

"I hope you are not tired of Swedish waffles."

"How could I be? But this morning, I'll take lingonberry jam without sugar or butter."

As soon as they finished breakfast, she pointed to the living room and his books. "Now, you can get back to your studies. There are several things I must do at the university. I will not be long."

After four hours, he'd completed the book Inga said was most important to his education. He had begun to fidget by the time she returned. "Are you finished already?" she asked. "So, let us see what you learned."

"Whoa. No exams, in case you've forgotten."

"No exams. Only a few friendly questions."

"Are friendly questions like friendly fire?"

She shook her head and laughed. After a few minutes of friendly questions and shaky answers, he got up. "Enough for now. I need a little fresh air."

"All right, but a short walk. You have more to read."

"When do you bring out the whip?"

"I hope you will not find out."

He walked to Kristianstad's shopping district and went into a bookstore, where he found several books in English, none of which interested him. He crossed the street to a shop selling original artwork. *Perfect*, he thought, admiring a display of paintings by a local artist. He purchased a watercolor of Saint Mary's Church in Åhus and had it gift wrapped. Back in her apartment, he laid it on the dining room table as she came in from the kitchen. "What is that?"

"It's only a small gift. Here." He handed her the brightly wrapped package.

She removed the paper and held up the painting. "Wonderful! Absolutely beautiful. I love the artist, and this is one of her finest works. And the Rundstrom family plot is in the Saint Mary's Church cemetery. Thank you, Cal."

"I'm glad you're happy."

"Now, Dr. Larsson, return to the sofa, and get back to your studies."

As she sat down and opened a book, Cal noticed the author's name—Stieg Larsson. "Which one is that?"

"In English, *The Girl with the Dragon Tattoo*. Have you read it?"

"All three of his *Millennium* trilogy. A shame he died so young."

After an hour, he asked, "How about a drink? I noticed a collection of interesting bottles in the kitchen."

"Absolut vodka, on the rocks for me. While you fix drinks, I will hang the painting. I know exactly where. Then we can eat." She grabbed a hammer and went into the living room.

Chapter 5

Wounded Thumb

Cal put the Absolut on the counter and was reaching for the scotch when he heard Inga. The urgency in her voice said drinks could wait. She was hunched over, shaking her left hand and glowering at the hammer lying on the floor.

"What's wrong?"

"Oh! Damn me … shit it … oh God, it hurts!"

"What happened?"

"I crushed my poor thumb, putting the hell's bells hook in the wall."

He looked away and made an unsuccessful effort to suppress a smile.

"What the damn Sam is so amusing about my pain?"

"I'm sorry, but I've never known anyone who cursed so poorly."

He heard her force a barely audible laugh. "I do much better in Swedish."

"Here, let me see what you did."

She jerked her hand away as he touched it.

"Nasty looking," he said, "but you might get a patent on that shade of purple."

"Are your stupid jokes meant to make my pain go away?"

"I apologize again. Let's find a professional. Something may be broken."

"That is not necessary. I shall live."

He ignored her protest and put on his jacket. "Where are the car keys?"

"On the table. But do not worry, I will be fine."

"Listen to the doctor."

"Yes, but I am listening to a rock doctor." She grinned and wrinkled her nose.

"The outpatient clinic on Mortsen is open twenty-four hours."

After a short drive, he pulled up at the entrance and stopped.

"I'll park and meet you inside."

The waiting room was empty, so he walked down the hall and found a nurse. "I'm with Miss. Rundstrom. How is she?"

"Fine, but still cursing about what she did to her thumb."

"In Swedish or English?"

"Swedish." The nurse snickered and led him back to the waiting room. "She'll meet you here in a few minutes."

When Inga entered into the room, he walked over and gently touched her hand. "How's the thumb?"

"We will live," she said, holding out her left hand, now sporting an impressive splint.

"Anything broken?"

"No, only bruising and pain, but I am giving the damned shit hammer to my brother for his birthday."

"I'm sorry about laughing at you earlier."

"I guess my cursing should be in Swedish." Inga looked at the magazine Cal had been reading and asked, "Planning a vacation?"

"This got me thinking about a trip."

"Good, but let us talk about it tomorrow. I would like to go home and put my feet up."

Back in the car, she turned and said, "Here is a thought. Your hotel is a mile from my apartment, and you will be there all day reading anyway. This is stupid, driving back and forth. You can use the second bedroom, if you do not mind sleeping with a computer."

"Fine." A computer hadn't been his first choice as a roommate, but now maybe he could get to know her.

"Good. Let's collect your things," she said.

"Are you sure you don't want to go straight to your apartment?"

"I can wait that long." As soon as the car began to move, she dozed off.

He parked in front of her apartment and opened the car door. Startled, she looked at him with sleepy eyes. "How did we get here so fast? Did we go to the hotel?"

"We did, and you slept the whole way."

He finished putting the picture hanger into the wall and hung the painting of Saint Mary's Church.

"It looks wonderful on that wall where I see it as soon as I come into the apartment. Would you like something to drink? A vodka martini, maybe?" she asked.

"Sounds good. The Absolut should still be on the counter. I'll get it."

"I will be back in a minute. I have something to do in the office."

He followed her and arrived in her office as she started to open the sofa bed. "Inga! Let me do that."

"My thumb and I appreciate that."

When he finished making his bed, they went back into the living room. "Why don't you sit on the sofa while I fix us those vodka martinis?"

"Now that I think about it, the doctor said no alcohol, but you go ahead." As she said this, her eyes began to flutter.

When he returned, she was asleep. He sat down, put his arm around her, and dozed off. He woke up early and decided to take a walk in the cool morning air. He met several people on their way to catch the tram, which ran in front of the apartment. He gave the only Swedish greeting he remembered from earlier visits to his cousins—*god middag*. They smiled and responded with a polite nod.

One elderly gentleman gave him a broad smile. "I do not wish to be rude, but you just wished me *good afternoon. God morgon* might be better, but I do appreciate your greeting in Swedish."

An attractive young woman in a business suit approached, so he tried again.

"*God morgon.*" She laughed. "Good morning to you. Please excuse me, but I love using English when I can."

He continued on, staring down at the disinterested sidewalk. *This is ridiculous*, he thought. *Before I visit my cousins, I'll have to work on my Swedish.*

He walked several blocks and then returned to Inga's building. A black Mercedes SUV was parked in front of it. *Damn! That looks like the SUV in the Absolut parking lot*, he thought as he strolled into a nearby park and found a bench with a clear view of the street. In a few minutes, the door opened, and a stocky woman got out. Even from two blocks away, her short spiky white hair and generous breasts caught his attention. She opened the rear door for a large German shepherd. It serviced unappreciative flowers in the nearby garden and sat next to the SUV. Maybe Inga had been right about being watched. Cal sat for another five minutes and was going to walk over for a closer look when the door opened. The dog jumped in, and Cal stepped back into the park, watching as the SUV pulled away. *That has to be the German shepherd and SUV Mark saw in Åhus, but is that woman following me or Inga, or both of us, and is this connected to Inga's concern about the research in her mysterious laboratory?*

The aroma of freshly brewed coffee greeted him in the apartment. Inga stood in front of the stove.

"American in the kitchen," he said.

"I know. I heard you come in. Where did you go? I feared you went back to the hotel after being exiled to my office."

"No; it is such a beautiful morning, I decided to have a look around the neighborhood." He considered telling her about what he'd just seen. *No, not now.*

"Last night, you mentioned taking a trip. Where were you thinking about going?"

"After I get back from visiting my cousins in Vasteras, how would a trip to Tuscany sound? Should have enough time before we leave for your laboratory."

"Well, I had not thought about going to Italy."

"Don't think about it. Just say yes. I'll plan everything and will be a first-rate guide, unless you're bored with Tuscany."

"That would not be possible; I toured Florence once in high school. Nothing more. Yes! A trip sounds like fun."

He embraced her, and when she didn't object, he nuzzled her neck. His hands slid across the smooth fabric of her nightgown until they came to her breasts. She leaned against him and sighed. Then without warning, her body stiffened and pulled away. He put his hands on her shoulders. For several minutes, neither of them moved. All he could see was the back of her head, but he knew she was crying. He tried to hold her, but she slipped away, dropping onto a kitchen chair. Her body shook, while tears fell in earnest.

He felt helpless and unable to think of anything to say, so he went to the bathroom and brought her some tissues. She dabbed her eyes and blew her nose. "Cal! I am sorry."

"No, I'm the one who's sorry. I shouldn't have touched you like that."

"I wanted you to. To hold me. To touch me." She must have recognized the confusion in his face, because she touched his cheek. "When you came over and put your hands on me, it made me happy and excited, but then the other me took over. That one was terrified."

"I want to understand, but it's difficult."

Her tears welled up again. "I am not being very helpful, am I? If there was only some way to explain."

"Inga, I—"

"No, let me start. I am not crazy. I have several psychiatrist friends at Lund who assure me I am not. It is a question I have often asked myself."

"Do you love someone else? Someone you can't let go of?" He felt embarrassed to ask this, given his feelings for Kara, and he wondered why romance had to be so complicated.

"No! No one."

"You're not …" He hesitated, uncertain how to continue.

"Am I lesbian?"

"Yes, I guess that's what I was trying to ask."

"Never in my life have I been attracted to women in such a way. You are committing a lot of time to me. This stupid studying, the trip to the lab, and now a trip to Italy. You are wonderful. I am grateful, but we should stop now. I can never be the woman for you."

"If you want me to go away, I will, but it's not my choice."

"Truly, I do not want you to go." She put her arms around his neck and kissed him.

You truly are a puzzle, he thought, *but I do enjoy being with you. I guess if you're not interested ... well, maybe someday.*

"Time to get to work," she said.

Cal looked at the new books she'd left on the table. After four hours, his face brightened. "Here's a chapter written by Dr. Ingegerd Marie Rundstrom. You?"

"Yes. I am so glad *Inga* stuck, not Ingegerd."

"You fibbed about Marie," he said.

Her eyebrows lifted, and she shrugged with a bemused smirk.

"It's been four hours since breakfast," he said, "and I'm afraid you'll have a cranky student here unless he gets something to eat."

"If you must eat, we should go."

They went to a small restaurant and ate sandwiches in silence.

※

Back in the apartment, he sat next to her on the sofa. "You've got to understand, I haven't been on this end of the academic seesaw for many years. It's not easy, and I apologize if I got whiny. How is the thumb?"

"I must admit, it still hurts like shit!" she said, smiling for the first time since breakfast. "Better, the way I used *shit*?"

"Better. Much better."

Is the aching thumb responsible for Inga's bad mood, or something deeper? Cal wondered. "I'll spend a few more hours with these books. After your friendly interrogation, we'll go for dinner and a movie."

The next morning, Cal was back at the coffee table reading. After several hours, he stretched and walked to the window. "I need some divine inspiration. Let's walk over to the church I saw down the street. It looks interesting."

"Too bad we don't have more seventeenth-century churches like it in America."

"You can take some of ours."

"Great! How about a few castles too?"

"Sorry; we keep the castles."

After they'd returned to the apartment, he started through the books with renewed energy.

"Must be something to divine inspiration. I would never have guessed. Read for a few more hours, and then I will fix a tasty pasta dish, with some Chianti. Good practice for Tuscany."

For two more days, he read and paced; Inga explained and asked questions. During his breaks, they wandered through Kristianstad. On his last day of "Immunology 101," he said, "I've learned as much of this as I'm going to."

"You have been a good student. You probably know more than is necessary."

"Good. Let's go so I can get my ticket to Vasteras."

At the train station, she pointed across the large waiting room. "Over there. I will find some coffee while you buy your tickets. Just tell them where you want to go; they will do the rest. As you know, English will not be a problem."

He joined her at a small table in the coffee shop. He examined the fistful of tickets. "All these for one trip?"

"Unfortunately, Vasteras is not on the main line ... lots of transfers. Do not worry; our trains run on time, and people love helping Americans. Your train from Stockholm back to Kristianstad will be easier."

"I'll make reservations for our plane tickets to Pisa online," Cal said.

As they were about to enter her apartment, Cal turned and caressed her cheek. "I'm going to miss you."

"I will miss you too."

Chapter 6

Vasteras Cousins

Early the next morning, Inga drove Cal to the station.

"Have a good time with your cousins." She leaned over and gave him a sisterly kiss on the cheek.

"Thanks. See you in a few days." He resisted the urge to respond with a passionate one.

"You had better hurry. This is the last train until noon." She grinned as if she'd read his mind.

He took a window seat and waved to her. *Larsson, you're such a wuss. Why didn't you give her a great big sloppy one? On the crowded platform, she probably wouldn't have made a scene.*

When the train pulled into the Vasteras station, he grabbed his bag and hurried out, because stops were brief and unforgiving. By the time he'd walked halfway down the platform, he saw Johanna and Gunnar. She broke into a run, greeting him with a warm hug.

"Marvelous to see you. I'm relieved you still have your beard. Brenda wrote you threatened to cut if off."

"Only a threat. How are you, Johanna?"

"As good as an old girl can be."

Gunnar, moving slower than his wife, reached Cal and gave him a vigorous handshake.

"Come," Gunnar said. "Let's get out of here. Hulda and Nils are coming for dinner. She and Johanna fixed you something special. Per Ake and Bjorn are away at university, so you'll stay with us on the lake."

"Perfect," Cal said, remembering their summer cottage on the shores of Lake Mälaren.

When they got to the house, Cal gazed at the reflection of the rounded hills across the lake. "It's even more beautiful than I remembered."

Gunnar nodded. "It is. Sometimes, I need someone to remind me."

Hulda and Nils arrived. They all sat at the massive oak table covered by plates of pickled herring, boiled new potatoes with fresh dill and sour cream, spare ribs, and grilled salmon. Later, Johanna and Hulda brought in bowls of cream and deep red strawberries from their gardens.

"A fabulous dinner fit for a king and a visiting cousin." Cal hugged the two sisters. "My first midsummer feast in years was wonderful."

"Would anyone go for a taste of schnapps?" Nils asked. "This is my contribution. A great help with digestion."

Cal nodded and retrieved the gifts from his bag. "I did a little shopping in Orrefors."

"This is lovely. Thank you, Cal! We understand you're no longer working," Nils said.

"True. Retired early, but I don't plan to vegetate. There are things I plan to do."

"Is getting a wife one of them?" Hulda asked.

"You're what … fifty-five? The sand is rushing through the hourglass. Don't you want children?" Johanna asked.

"You're as bad as Hulda," Gunner said.

"Brenda's daughters are my children. I'm going to Tuscany with a beautiful Swedish lady from Kristianstad. Inga's intelligent, fun to be with, and not married."

"Why didn't you tell us in the first place? Sounds promising," Gunnar said.

"Perhaps, but she has a problem with what goes on in the laboratory where she works and wants me to help her figure it out."

"What kind of problem?" Nils asked.

"Not sure. She's quite secretive, but I've seen things that make me think that the problem is real, and she may be in danger."

They glanced at each other and gave a collective Swedish shrug.

Nils's relentless interrogation continued. "How do you get on with her?"

"We enjoy being together. The problem is whenever I get romantic—try to kiss her, touch her—she pushes me away. She's like one of those hermit crabs down at the beach. Stand away, and the small crab crawls out of the shell it carries on its back. Attempt to pick it up, and it darts back into the shell. She's my beautiful hermit crab. Every time I think she's left her shell and I make a romantic gesture, she runs. I'm at a loss to understand why."

"If she knows you compare her to a crab, that might be your problem." Nils laughed. "Cal, you surely have plans other than romance."

"I've been thinking a lot about what I'll do when I get home. I may take painting classes at the university."

"I thought you retired. That is hard work, going up and down ladders." Nils waved his hand with an invisible paintbrush.

They all laughed.

After days of sightseeing and evenings spent eating, drinking, and enjoying his cousins, Cal boarded the train for the trip to Stockholm. He regretted the stay had been so short, although the prospect of being with Inga invigorated him.

The train to Stockholm got him to his hotel early enough to call several people on the list Mark had given him. Later, he saw two possible clients who might be interested in studies of limestone.

On the final day, he had one morning appointment and spent the afternoon cruising through the Stockholm archipelago to Sandhamn. Relaxing in the warm sun, he thought about Nils's question. It forced him to revisit the something he'd yet to answer. What now? Golf in Pinehurst, a few miles from his house, could be fun but would eventually get boring. Talking with Mark's friends convinced him consulting wasn't in his future. He'd already spent too many years staring through the microscope. His pension meant he didn't need a paying job. He was relatively young and healthy, but what would he do? Painting and photography? For now, Inga and her mysterious problem would keep him busy. In time, he'd figure out the rest.

    Back in the city, he caught the train to Kristianstad. There were no transfers, and he slept soundly for three hours, napping in the station until Inga arrived.

Chapter 7

Hermit Crab Comes out of Her Shell

On the nearly empty train platform, Inga met Cal with an embrace, mirrored by other middle-aged couples acting out the same morning ritual. They found a table, and Inga pulled two large Styrofoam cups from a paper bag.

"Coffee and muffins?" she asked.

"Thanks. It's so early—where did you get this?"

"The shop in the station, where we had pastries the other day. How are your cousins?"

"Fine. Everyone was there except the boys, who are still at university."

"Did you have success in Stockholm?"

"I met with the people Mark recommended, and we talked about consulting. Studying limestone and looking for high-porosity zones could be interesting, but it's not for me right now."

"What are you going to do after you get home?"

"For now, travel, fun research, or play artist. Maybe all three."

"Won't you get bored?"

"If that happens, I'll spend more time with a gorgeous Swedish lady I met recently."

She smiled and kissed him. "Your beard tickles."

"You could get used to it."

"I might try. I am quite happy, you know. Happier than I have been in a long time."

"So am I," he said.

This caught the attention of a young couple. The girl stage-whispered to her boyfriend. He pulled her along and answered, not attempting to be quiet.

She released his hand and stomped off.

Cal heard the conversation but didn't understand a word. "Did I miss something interesting?"

Inga giggled. "She thinks it is cute, an old couple, like us, could be romantic. He said you are probably my boss trying to get into my pants. That made her angry, as you saw."

Giggling wasn't her style, but Cal found it charming anyway.

"Old couple like us?"

"Yes. I guess to them, everyone over thirty is old."

Later, after a light supper in Inga's apartment, they packed for Italy. She dozed as they watched television. Cal looked over at her, her lashes brushing the tops of her cheeks. *She looks so peaceful*, he thought, *so calm.* Her brow furrowed just slightly as she dreamed. *Damn, I wish I knew what was on her mind, why she is being followed and what frightens her.*

The flight from Copenhagen to Pisa took less time than the drive to its iconic tower. He drove through the narrow streets filled with people, motor scooters, baby carriages, old men pushing carts. "Absolutely insane," he muttered to himself. Driving in congested cities, especially Italian cities, brought out the worst in him, but there was no point getting the trip off to a bad start, he thought. Congratulating himself on not losing his temper, he glanced at Inga and noticed her eyes were shut. "Taking a nap?"

"No. This traffic makes me nervous, and I prefer not to watch." She laughed and opened her eyes enough to wink at him.

"I'm sorry we have to start our trip like this, but welcome to Italy from a car. The worst will be behind us, and it's worth the trouble to see the tower at least once. Ah, at last," he said as Pisa's celebrated landmark emerged from a jumble of unremarkable buildings. He parked, and they approached the tower, where a sign announced CLOSED FOR REPAIRS.

"Damn! The bloody thing is never open. Tried several times, but never have made it to the top—or, for that matter, past the first step. I should have known since there's no crowd."

"Do not be cross. The truth is—I am happier here on the ground. That seems to be open. Shall we go in?" she asked, pointing to the Romanesque cathedral crouching beside the tower.

"Let's."

They joined the line of tourists streaming into the massive cathedral. "I guess when the tower's closed, business here picks up."

An hour later, returning to the sunny Italian afternoon, she blinked and turned back to look at the building they'd just left. "So spectacular on the outside, and inside rather somber, but I am still glad we saw it."

⚜

Inga napped during the drive to Lucca. She didn't rouse until they had passed through the city gate. "How did you get this far without running over anyone?"

"In Italy, you sort of get used to it. Drive slowly, and come with a decent supply of curse words, but most importantly, drive like they do." He swerved to avoid a bicycle and beat a Fiat to the last available parking space in the tiny parking lot next to the Hotel Porta Rossa. Their third-floor suite was furnished with elegant antiques and had a wide balcony facing the Piazza Napoleone. The sofa bed had been pulled out, waiting to perform its alternative function.

"I'll sleep here. You take the bedroom," Cal said, nodding toward the door on the far side of the large sitting room.

"Not necessary. I will take the sofa."

"No, I prefer this, so I can enjoy the piazza."

"If that is what you want." She sidled up to him. The faint scent of perfume and the closeness of her body made him forget the drive into the city.

Their lips nearly met, when the porter arrived with their luggage. "*Mi scusi*," he said, obviously embarrassed.

"*Grazie.*" Cal gave him a rueful smile and two euros.

"*Prego.*" He nodded and made a quick exit.

Cal realized the moment was lost. Which was the real Inga? The one greeting him on the train platform like a wife of thirty years, or this one whose touch and aroma he found so exciting? The latter, he hoped.

"It will be three hours before the restaurants open for dinner," he said. "Let's go for a walk."

They crossed the Piazza Napoleone and wandered down a narrow street to the Piazza dell'Anfiteatro. "I see the sign, but where is the piazza?"

"This way." Soon they reached a tunnel covered by a low arch. On the other side, they emerged in an oval space ringed by yellow buildings with red-tiled roofs.

"Extraordinary! But why this shape?"

"Two thousand years ago, this was a Roman amphitheater."

"With lots of nice shops now. Do we have time?"

"We'll make time."

She bought a selection of colorful silk scarves. "For my sisters; they will love these. How about your sister and nieces?"

"Yes. Would you help me pick out a few?"

"Of course."

Together they filled a bag.

"These are perfect. Thank you," he said.

They strolled down the street, stopping at the fourteenth-century redbrick Torre Guinigi.

"The view of the city is splendid from up there," he said, pointing to the top of the building.

"Are those live trees?"

"Yes. There's a garden of small oaks growing on the top of a medieval tower. Once there were hundreds of towers like this. Torre Guinigi is one of the survivors. Do you want to go up? It's only eight stories to the rooftop terrace. There is an elevator, or we can walk up."

"I need some exercise," she said. "Let's use the stairs."

Then he remembered the 230 steps between them and the garden. When he finally got to the last step, Inga stood waiting. "Do you run up lots of stairs at the university?" he panted.

"No, but I do walk a lot. That was an important part of the therapy after my riding injury. I used to have a bad limp, but now it is nearly gone," she answered as she went through the door to the garden. "The terracotta rooftops and mountains are magnificent." She took several photos with her smartphone and stroked a huge ceramic vase perched on a low wall at the edge of the terrace. "I would love to have one of these."

Cal grinned. "Six feet tall and a hundred pounds. I think the scarves are better. They will fit in the plane's overhead. Come to North Carolina. I have a potter friend who makes colossal vases, but prettier than these." He looked across the garden to a small bar that he remembered from an earlier visit. "Best martinis in Tuscany, but it seems to be closed." He stood at the wall, watching as the sun sank closer to the horizon, turning the clouds to nature's palette of fiery reds and oranges. Movement in the street made him wish he had binoculars. He glimpsed someone who resembled the white-haired woman he'd seen in the black SUV near Inga's apartment, but he decided his imagination was working overtime in the failing light.

"What is the matter?" Inga slipped her hand into his.

He didn't answer her question, because he didn't want to unsettle her. "It looks like the bar here is closed. Let's go find a drink."

"I think we should take the elevator this time," she said.

"Bless you, my child."

She laughed, pushing the button that would spare him 230 more steps.

Back on the ground, they turned to admire Torre Guinigi, when the woman who'd sold them the tickets for the tower ran to the street yelling. On instinct, Cal pulled Inga to one side. A large vase hit the pavement, spraying them with shards of broken pottery.

The woman who had yelled the warning ran over. "Is anyone injured? Oh God. Nothing like that has ever happened before. Oh sweet Jesus. Did any of those pieces hurt you?"

He put a hand on Inga's trembling arm. "We're fine. No one's hurt, but that was lucky."

"I told the fools to secure the pots or remove them!" she screamed, arms waving Italian-style to better emphasize the drama.

"They may listen to you now." He turned to Inga, still visibly shaken. "Are you okay? I'll bet they'll let you can keep a piece of the vase as a souvenir. They're everywhere."

She shook her head emphatically. "No, they stay in Lucca. I will come to North Carolina and get an unbroken one from your friend."

One hell of a coincidence, Cal thought. *A white-haired woman and a falling vase.* No one else was up there when they were, but someone could have gone up the stairs while they came down in the elevator. He turned, looked up at the tower's garden, and shook his head. "Let's hike the city walls. Can't holiday in Lucca without doing that," he said, putting his arm around her.

They strolled along the tree-lined promenade on top of the massive sixteenth-century ramparts as darkness brought an unexpected chill. He looked down onto the street they'd just left. In the gloom, he thought he saw someone with a large dog. "What the shit? That can't be her again," he whispered.

"What's wrong?" she asked.

"It's nothing, but you have to be careful of pickpockets."

Her arched eyebrow asked without words, *What aren't you telling me?*

He wasn't sure how to answer her unspoken question. He took her hand, and they began walking back to their hotel.

"Enough walking for the day," Inga said as they went up to their room. "Shall we eat? The restaurants seem to be open."

"Sounds good. Do you need some time?" he asked.

"Give me a second. I want to change into something fresh."

Inga came out wearing a pink silk blouse with one of her new scarves. She seemed different, but he couldn't put his finger on how.

"Time for that famous Tuscan food," she said.

They went into Il Cedro, a restaurant on the piazza, and took a table next to the window. Cal watched Inga, now totally absorbed by the view of the Piazza Napoleone. Then he noticed how the silk blouse clung to her body with an unmistakable message. *Her bra is back in the hotel.* The waiter wasn't so slow to recognize Inga's new look.

"Could I bring you wine?" he asked, giving Inga his full attention.

"Yes. Chianti Classico would be fine," Cal said.

"My pleasure," he answered. "We get many tourists, but few so lovely as the lady." He seemed reluctant to leave the table, until Cal cleared his throat to send him on his way.

"I've only been here one day; I adore Tuscany." She smiled at Cal.

"And Tuscany seems to adore you."

The Bistecca alla Fiorentina, topped off with Ricciarelli, was the perfect ending for their first day in Italy.

"That food was so good. I am stuffed; you may have to carry me back to the hotel. What was that marvelous dessert?"

"Ground orange peel and almonds with honey, I think."

As they were leaving, the waiter trotted over and held the door. "Allow me, goddess from the north."

"Goddess from the north—that is charming." She laughed as they left the restaurant and returned to crowded street.

"He's good with accents." Cal tried to be less obvious than he'd been earlier as he scanned the street.

Once they were back in their suite, she gave him a light kiss on the lips. "Thank you for a divine evening." She slipped past him into the bedroom. Then he heard the shower.

This is one complicated woman, he thought, lying on his sofa turned bed.

The next morning when Cal opened his eyes, he saw brushstrokes of pink and lavender lightening the morning sky. Then he noticed that the balcony door was open. Inga sat on one of the lounge chairs, taking in the piazza at sunrise. He got up and put on the pants and shirt he'd dropped on the floor the night before.

"Good morning, Cal. I hope that I did not wake you."

"No, you didn't. When did you come out here?"

"Midnight, I think. I could not get to sleep." Turning to face him, her robe slipped to the floor. Even in the half-light, he could see every curve and recess. She got up, walked over, and put her arms around his neck. She pressed her mouth hard against his, and they enjoyed a moment of exploration.

"Your bed or mine?" he asked.

"Mine is queen size … more room to play."

Later, he lay on his side, captivated by her beauty. She rolled over to face him, allowing unruly curls to tumble around her face. "Shall we play a little longer? The sun is just coming up."

The clock rang ten as Cal arrived in the lobby. He bought an English-language newspaper and found a comfortable chair to wait while Inga dressed. The paper was mostly advertising and stories concerning events for the upcoming day. He was about to put it down when he noticed an article at the bottom of the page. A body had been found in the tower on Via Sant'Andrea. It was a part-time bartender whose neck was broken in what the police called an unfortunate accident. Cal realized immediately this was the Torre Guinigi, where they'd been the day before, and it explained why the bar had not been open.

He grimaced. Was it an unfortunate accident, like the vase that nearly killed them? They were probably there when this happened, and so was the woman with white hair. Inga had reason to be afraid.

The fräulein waited for him to answer his phone. "Pick up, you fool. I haven't got all day." As the phone in another part of Lucca continued to ring, she became increasingly agitated, causing other patrons in the café to stare. "I know you're on the phone; I hear you breathing. I saw what happened yesterday; you are so stupid. My dear brother, if anything happens to Inga, you will die in the most painful way possible. She is mine now and forever, but if you want to kill the American, don't let me stop you." She reached down and stroked the large German shepherd, which looked up with unfeeling eyes. "You would see that we keep her safe, won't you, my little friend?"

The drive to San Gimignano didn't take long. As the medieval towers came into view, she touched his arm. "How could we have not come here? Dazzling, with uncounted shades of gray, umber, and sienna. I am happy you suggested it."

"The fourteen towers and I are happy you appreciate them."

"Can we stop?"

"Do you think we'd get this close and not stop? Plenty of good places for lunch and excellent shops with Tuscan jewelry and art."

They found a small restaurant and enjoyed a glass of Chianti with bread and antipasto.

They'd only gone a few feet when Inga stopped. "Oh, I love those blue napkins," she said, disappearing into one of the many gift shops on San Gimignano's famous hill.

"I'll meet you here in fifteen minutes," he said and continued on to his favorite jewelry store in Italy.

When they met at the fabric shop, she had a large shopping bag.

"Who is that for?" Cal asked.

"Me," she said, pulling out a beautiful, sapphire-colored napkin.

"Good for you. It's just right."

"Did you buy anything?"

"No, simply window-shopping," he said. "Time to go. Colle di Val d'Elsa closes in three hours."

Cal drove out of the parking lot and turned southeast toward Colle di Val d'Elsa.

"Did you see the monster parked next to us?" Inga asked.

"Sort of. Enough to know it was much too big for these narrow roads."

"No, I meant the person standing next to it. He was enormous and not at all pleasant looking. Like Dr. Frankenstein's creature in those terrible movies my brother, Frederick, loves. I always hated those movies and found that person to be very frightening."

"Sorry, but I didn't see him," Cal snapped, now fully preoccupied with their Corolla. The brakes were mushy. He was sure they had been fine earlier.

After two blocks, the road descended into the Il Rosolaccio Valley. The only thing ahead of them was a farm truck loaded with melons. *With all these curves, passing him is going to be a bitch*, he thought as he tapped the brakes. "Shit! Nothing! They're gone."

Inga turned to face him. "What is happening?"

"The damned brakes are gone."

The Corolla accelerated, and soon the slow farm truck was only a few feet ahead of them. Cal managed to steer around it.

"Cal! What are you doing?"

"I have no brakes. Hang on!"

They skidded around a sharp curve. Inga was thrown against the door, and the scenery she'd been enjoying was now a terrifying blur. With each curve, Cal had less control of the car.

"Slow down. Please!" She braced against the dashboard.

"I wish I could." He managed to shift to a lower gear. The bottom of the hill came into view as they rounded the last curve. "We're nearly down—might just make it in one piece."

Now on flat ground, the car roared through a dilapidated Shell station, barely missing the gas pumps, coming to an abrupt stop deep in a thicket of tall weeds and even taller flowers.

As they got out of the car in a cloud of dust and pollen, a grizzled old man stormed out of the office, hollering in Italian, oblivious to Cal's equally emotional explanation in English.

A young man wearing greasy overalls ran to join them. "Father doesn't speak English and can't understand why you parked in his flower garden."

"Tell him I'm sorry. I lost my brakes coming down the hill and will pay for any damages."

The young man translated as the old man waved his arms and stalked back into his office.

"Let's check your car and see why it did such a stupid thing," the mechanic said.

They pushed the car to a service bay, and he slid under the car. Before long, he produced a small black rubber hose. "This carries the brake fluid from the master cylinder to your brakes."

"It's broken. Why? This is a new car."

"Cut. Not broken. See here? The edge is smooth."

"How long ago?"

"Not long. Probably no more than an hour."

Cal looked at Inga, who was still shaking after the harrowing ride. He didn't know how to explain and decided to give her something to do so he could think. "Would you do me a big favor and go to the restaurant next door and get a couple of cappuccinos?"

As she started to leave, he yelled after her, "And two extras for our friends!"

"Let me get started. Won't take long to fix, but in the future, you might keep an eye on your car."

The melon truck came by, and the driver gave Cal an instantly recognizable gesture with his left hand.

The mechanic laughed and with great enthusiasm returned it. "You did seem to upset someone."

"Can't say I blame him." Cal grimaced.

"Here are the cappuccinos," Inga said, returning with four steaming drinks.

"*Grazie*," the mechanic said with a dip of the head.

"Would you give one to the old gentleman in the office? Might take his mind off the flowers."

"Yes. I am sure he is not pleased with our car's lovely bouquets. What happened to the car?" she asked.

"The little hose that carries the brake fluid was cut."

"How can such a thing happen? Did someone do it to hurt us? And when did they do it?"

"All good questions. Who, why, or when? I don't know."

"Could it have been the terrible-looking giant parked next to us in San Gimignano?"

"What kind of car was it?"

"Just a big black car. Mercedes, maybe," she answered.

"An SUV?"

"Yes. That is what they are called."

Too many black SUVs, Cal thought. *The white-haired woman and her dog, now a menacing giant. Is all this related to the death of the bartender in the tower or the sabotage to their car?* He was brought back to the present when the mechanic approached with a bill.

"I replaced the line and the brake fluid. You are ready to go."

"I appreciate it. Thank you," Cal said, and he handed the mechanic money for the repair and the ruined garden. "Only a few scratches on the bumper. Hope they don't notice when I return it to the rental agency."

"You will remind them of their broken hose that nearly got us killed," Inga said, rejoining him at the car.

"Don't think I'll mention it, as it was cut, and I'm sure the rental people didn't do the cutting. We'd best get back on the road." He tested the brakes as he pulled out of the service station. They waved to the mechanic and his father. "Look at that! The old guy returned our wave; he even smiled. Guess the cappuccino did the trick."

"The fifty-euro weed payment helped, I am sure," she said with a chuckle.

Even though he was looking forward to Colle di Val d'Elsa's glass, his mind couldn't leave the parking lot in San Gimignano and the harrowing ride that followed.

The drive to Colle di Val d'Elsa took less than an hour. They went up the stairs to Cristalleria Laica's showroom, with its extravagant display of crystal glass—the best in Italy—but neither could generate any enthusiasm. Cal picked up a delicate lavender decanter, barely seeing it. He ran a finger tenderly across a stunning blue iridescent bowl and shook his head.

"Damn. My hearts not in this," he said quietly. "Too bad; I love this stuff." He took Inga's hand and nodded toward the exit. "Shall we go?"

With a half smile, she blinked, and they returned to their car.

Chapter 8

A Room in Siena

Cal drove up the hill to a parking garage outside Siena's medieval city walls.

"We'll park here. Let's leave the bags and explore before everything closes." He glanced at his watch. "I hope we get to the cathedral before they lock up."

Laughing, she took his hand. "If you want to hurry, let us hurry."

After ten minutes of running, he stopped short and looked around.

"What's wrong?" she asked. "Was I moving too fast?"

"No. I'm turned around, and I left the damned map in the car."

"I cannot read Italian, but that sign says the Piazza del Duomo is up there." She pointed to the street they'd just passed. "That is where we are going. Right?"

He nodded. As they started up the hill toward the duomo, Cal's attempts to shake off the events of the past several days were futile. *A black SUV with a white-haired woman and her large dog that seem to be everywhere,* he thought. *Is she the one who tried to kill us with the falling vase at Lucca's Torre Guinigi and sabotaged the brakes before we left San Gimignano? If so, is this connected to Inga's concerns about the research in the laboratory where she works?*

"You wanted to hurry. Let us hurry." She grabbed his hand and pulled him into the piazza. She paused and gazed at the ornate duomo towering above them. "Oh, Cal, this is fabulous."

They stood admiring the thirteenth-century cathedral, one of the great masterpieces of Italian architecture. "Yes. It is something, isn't it?" he said, glad he'd brought her here.

"The facade is breathtaking. The alternating stripes of white marble and black marble are unbelievably exquisite." She leaned against him.

"The interior is even better. Let's go," he said.

They hurried across the broad piazza in front of the duomo.

Inside, her eyes were drawn to the nave's vaulted ceiling with golden ribs separated by islands of green-and-gold mosaics. She gasped, "Magnificent." They'd only been inside only a few minutes before the attendants began locking the doors.

"Beautiful as it is, I'm afraid we must go," he said.

They returned to the piazza and looked back at the intricate spires and banding of black and white marble.

"You approve of today's brief Siena tour?"

She nodded and held his arm.

After a short walk, they reached their hotel. "Home for the night. I'll register. Then we'll get something to eat and retrieve the bags later."

The restaurant recommended by the desk clerk exceeded expectations. While they waited for the wine, he pulled a small package out of his pocket and laid it on the table in front of her.

"What is this?"

"Open it and find out."

She unwrapped the small box and removed the Etruscan earrings he had bought in San Gimignano, each a delicate hoop connected by corded gold wire encrusted with tiny gold beads.

"They are lovely." She leaned across the table and kissed him, blinking away a tear.

"I'm glad you like them."

She put them on and turned her head. "How do they look?"

"Nearly as beautiful as the woman wearing them. Shall we order? How does pasta sound?"

"Pasta sounds wonderful."

Dinner arrived; the waiter smiled at Inga. "What lovely earrings. A gift?"

"Yes. Pretty, aren't they?" She reached across the table and squeezed Cal's hands.

After the dinner plates were cleared, Cal said, "We still have to get our bags from the car." He wished now that they had done it earlier.

They walked hand in hand down the empty street toward the parking garage.

After several minutes, she whispered, "Do you hear something?"

He stopped and listened. "Footsteps. Probably tourists out for a stroll. It's a pleasant enough evening."

She shook her head. "Did you not say in Lucca that we should be concerned about pickpockets? Let us hurry."

"Here's the room key. Why don't you go on back to the hotel? It's just across the street. I'll get the bags."

"I will stay with you. I do not want you getting mugged alone."

"Okay, so we'll get mugged together." Cal meant this as a joke but found it more ominous than he cared to admit.

After the short walk to the car, they retrieved their suitcases. He stood looking at Inga, who had heard them too.

"More footsteps," she said.

"Can you run in those heels?"

"I will try." They'd just started, when she stumbled. "Stupid shoes," she said, kicking them off.

Cal picked them up and grabbed her hand. "Let's move!"

Back in the hotel lobby, she stared at him with eyes red from too much Tuscan sun and too little sleep. "I am sure someone followed us tonight," Inga said.

"I never saw anyone. Probably just sightseers out for a breath of air. Sometimes, I think you worry too much." Cal hoped his face didn't reveal how he really felt as he pushed the elevator button. When nothing happened, he turned to Inga. "I'll put my bag behind the counter and retrieve it after you get settled." He took her bag, and they walked up the three flights of stairs.

Inside their room, he laid her suitcase on the luggage rack and returned to the lobby. When he got back, he found her sprawled across the bed, sound asleep. She'd managed to shed her clothes before exhaustion won. He covered her with a brightly colored comforter.

So much for tonight's game plan, he thought.

After breakfast and a visit to the Piazza del Campo, they loaded their Toyota and left Siena. "I am glad you are driving," she said. "The road is so crooked. It makes me nervous."

"This could be fun if I'd rented a Porsche."

"I am very happy you did not think of that earlier."

When San Galgano finally came into view, Inga gave her brow a theatrical smack with the back of her hand. Exhaling for added effect, she said, "We made it."

"Oh, please! It wasn't that bad."

"I am teasing. Might be fun to run it in a sports car."

"The Porsche I didn't rent." he grinned.

She smiled. "Yes, that Porsche."

As he pulled into the parking lot, he saw a black Mercedes SUV nearly hidden behind a tour bus. *This is stretching coincidence past the breaking point*, he thought. *Clearly her fears are well founded. If she is being followed and someone is trying to kill her, why?* Maybe it was time to end their trip, or was he just being the worrywart his sister accused him of being?

"I see the remains of a large building, but what is it?"

He looked at the decaying walls. "San Galgano. The ruins of a thirteenth-century Cistercian abbey, built by the same monks who oversaw construction of Siena's duomo. The stone walls are nearly intact, but the roof collapsed several hundred years ago." He hoped she hadn't noticed his preoccupation with what he'd seen in the parking lot, and knew he should be more honest with what he saw or thought he saw. *Damn*, he thought, *if only there was someplace where I could see the whole area. There are just too many places for someone to hide.*

"What is the round building on the hill?" she asked.

He continued staring back toward the parking lot.

"Cal, what is the matter? You are as edgy as a rat on a hot tin roof."

"Actually, that would be a 'cat,' but never mind." He tried to laugh. "I'm sorry; it's really nothing. Maybe the curves got to me more than I thought." He nodded toward the hill. "It's a small chapel. We'll go up in a minute, but first let's take a quick look in the abbey."

They entered the roofless Gothic nave, surrounded by cypresses and fields of yellow sunflowers. Its tall arched windows, set in the walls of gray travertine stone and red Sienese brick, provided a playground for the swallows swirling overhead.

"Churches never particularly fascinated me. This might change after the duomo and San Galgano," she said.

"Good, but there's something really interesting in the chapel. Let's hurry."

On the way up the hill, they passed lush vineyards and groves of large oaks. He peered into the deep shadows the trees cast, expecting movement that never came. He felt guilty about the worried look she'd worn since they arrived in San Galgano. Neither spoke as they approached the chapel.

"This seems to have survived better than the abbey," she said as they entered the round building. In its low alcoves, faded thirteenth- and fourteenth-century religious frescos depicted scenes from the life of Saint Galgano Guidotti. "At last! Something in English I can read. The people who made this display are unusually thoughtful of non-Italians."

Cal motioned for her to join him. "This is an interesting character. Before Guidotti became a monk, he was a knight. After his family and fellow knights tried to convince him he should return to his old life, he stuck his sword into a rock, renouncing his former career."

"Good story. Where is the sword now? Locked away in the Vatican archives?"

"Come." He led her to a hole in the chapel floor.

Beneath their feet, a sword's handle stuck out of a large rock. "Saint Galgano Guidotti's sword."

"Do not be silly. What is it really?"

"You surely have read the story of King Arthur and Excalibur?"

"A lovely legend. Please do not tell me you believe it.'

"I sure would love to examine this sword. Take a slice of stone near the blade and hit the area with ground-penetrating radar. That would tell us a lot, but obviously isn't going to happen. In the end, I'm left with the mystery of Saint Galgano Guidotti's sword."

"I guess this skeptical Swede must also believe in the mystery of Saint Galgano Guidotti's sword too."

"Good! Scientists need a little mystery in their lives. We should get on the road. We're spending the night on a working farm; the family has modified it to accommodate tourists. I've been there several times. Once I spent a month and made some pretty decent paintings. Last time I visited, one was still hanging in the office."

They reached the farm well after dark. Cheri Topham, a Yorkshire woman who managed the visitors' side of the business, greeted him with a hug. "Good to see you again, Cal. Haven't stayed with us for a while. Did you bring your watercolors? I love the painting you gave us. What was it, five years ago?"

"Something like that. No paints this time, but I brought a friend, Inga Rundstrom. Will she do?"

Cheri chuckled and greeted her like an old friend. "So nice to meet you, Inga."

"Sorry we're late, but driving from San Galgano took longer than I remembered," Cal said.

As they chatted, Cheri led them up the lane to their apartment.

"Any place where we can find some food at this hour?" Cal asked.

"Why don't you check the fridge?"

The small refrigerator overflowed with cold cuts, cheese, and white wine. Bread and red wine sat on the counter.

"This should hold you till morning." Cheri said.

"You're a wonder! This could feed us for days," Cal said.

After they took their bags into the bedroom, Inga explored the apartment. Cheri motioned for Cal to follower her outside.

"Well, it took long enough, but seems worth the wait. She's lovely."

"Something, isn't she?"

"Something indeed. Well, good night, Cal." She blew him a kiss as she headed down the path to the main house. "See you tomorrow."

He went back into the apartment. Cheri's comments reminded him just how smitten he'd become.

"What do you think? Is this as good as a Hilton?" he asked.

Inga laughed. "This is better than any Hilton I have stayed in. A huge bedroom, living room, kitchen, and dining room. Just look at those fabulous oak beams. What a place for a vacation. How did Cheri end up here?"

"Married one of the owners. Let's eat some of Cheri's banquet."

After finishing their late-night snack, he took a bottle of red wine to the patio. Inga sat beside him on a bench and rested her head on his shoulder as they enjoyed the warm breeze blowing across the valley.

"Can you tell me how you got the job in the laboratory we're going to see?" he asked.

"One day, a letter came to me at the university asking if I would be interested in a laboratory involved in cutting-edge research. I never heard of the person who signed it, but ReStemCo is a real company. I checked online and wanted something different for a while, so I decided this might be what I needed."

"What did you do?"

"I sent an e-mail telling them I would be willing to visit at the lab and talk with them."

"And?"

"A day later, I received an airline ticket and flew to the laboratory. I was there for three days and immediately realized it was state of the art. They offered me a year's contract at triple my salary. The research seemed stimulating. I had an unusually light schedule coming up, so I arranged for a leave of absence."

"Can you tell me now what goes on in the lab?"

She hesitated, staring at whatever hid in the dark shadows beyond the patio.

Cal's eye contact never wavered as he patiently waited for an answer.

She dropped her chin. "We create giant embryos."

"What? Why?"

"For embryonic stem cells."

"Your laboratory gets more and more interesting. How do they do that?"

"You must wait and see the lab to understand. The day I left for home, the laboratory's top security person spoke with me. Before joining ReStemCo, he had been a policeman in Texas. Houston, I think. His accent is difficult. I sometimes cannot understand him. A debriefing, he called it. Really more of a threat, I would say. He warned me not to tell anyone what goes on in the lab. From the first day, I found him a menacing person. He is a bully and seems to enjoy scaring people."

"So this is why you were so secretive?"

"Yes. That was why I did not want to meet you in Kristianstad, why we met in Åhus. I have become more and more concerned about what goes on in the laboratory."

"Why don't you walk away from it?"

"The pay is excellent, and in a bizarre way, the work is exciting, but I needed to talk to someone before I gave it all up. Cal, you became that someone."

He realized the tension in her voice was spreading through her body, so he stood up and patted the bench. "Here, lie down." He gently massaged her back until he felt her relax. "I can see how troubling this must be for you, but how can I help?"

He heard a low sigh as she rolled over. "I do not want to think about the lab now. Let us go inside."

Chapter 9

Morning Fog and Two Etruscan Lovers

Inga took refuge behind her pillow. "Why are you shaking me?"

"Come outside and look."

"When did your watch go missing?"

"I know it's early, but you'll thank me." He took her hand and tugged until they stood on the patio.

"I am freezing." With arms drawn tightly across her chest, she continued muttering in Swedish with a vocabulary he couldn't translate but knew might disturb his female cousins.

"Whatever happened to your Viking blood?"

"Why do you think so many Scandinavians moved to the States? They hated the cold."

"If true, they hired a lousy travel agent. Minnesota is a long way from warm weather."

Inga's expression showed no trace of amusement.

Cal went inside and returned with an eiderdown comforter, which he draped across her shoulders. "Better?"

"I suppose, but please explain why we are standing out here in the cold."

"Patience," he said, pointing toward the night sky being transformed by silver streaks. As the sun rose, black hills covered by oaks and slender cypress trees emerged from gray fog like islands rising from an undulating inland sea. Cal found the scene magical, like some abstract painting coming to life. "Aren't you pleased I you got up?" he asked.

"Enchanted! I am deliriously happy you dragged me out of a cozy, warm bed to freeze in the dark." She saw his disappointment. "I am sorry. It is lovely, but you must understand, I am not a morning person."

Cal acknowledged this with a hug. "Today is going to be a long one, so I'm afraid we should get dressed and go into town. La Pasticceria's cappuccino is the best in Tuscany; they open soon. We'll pack later. We can stay until noon."

When they got to town, the pastry shop had just opened. They each ordered panforte and biscotti, with steaming mugs of cappuccino.

"Tell me more about the place where we stayed last night," Inga said. "Seems to be prosperous."

"I'm sure it is. They own three thousand acres; it has been in the same family for generations. They grow grapes and olives. The apartment we were in is above the olive presses, which they still use. In the spring and summer, Cheri organizes classes in Tuscan cooking."

"The fog in the valley this morning was extraordinary. In spite of my whining, I did enjoy watching the hill sitting like an island in the fog. I am surprised you did not take any pictures."

"Normally, I would, but this time, a beautiful blonde occupied my attention. That's never happened before. One must make choices. You were mine."

"Flatterer. How about a redhead or brunette?"

"Never. Ask Cheri. Let's pick up some cheese, meat, and a bottle of wine. The shop up the street makes excellent bread. We'll have a picnic lunch."

"I like that idea, but when this trip ends, I will have to go on a yearlong diet."

They returned to the apartment and loaded the car. Cal motioned down the hill. "Let's take a short hike; the countryside is incredible. Cheri said we can park here for as long as we like."

"Shall we bring the food?"

"No. We'll be back before noon. There's a long drive ahead of us."

They walked along a winding road leading away from the agricultural estate's cluster of buildings. Tall, slender cypresses lined the sienna-stained road. Groves of squat olive trees with mysterious gnarled trunks competed with vineyards for space near the estate. After two miles, they passed through a stand of oaks and down a steep slope to a small river.

"This would be a grand place for a swim if the day were warmer," she said. "What is its name?"

"The Merse. I'm grateful you feel it's too cold. I didn't bring a wetsuit."

"Did you never take off your clothes and jump into a river?"

"Have you forgotten I'm an American? What about you?"

"Many times."

"You know, it sounds like a good idea after all."

She snickered and pulled him along a trail down to the river. Settling on a large rock, she fondled the gold Etruscan earrings. "I love them. No man has ever given me anything like them. Some tried to give me jewelry and nice presents, but I rejected them ... always pushed them away." Sadness spread across her face the way the morning's fog had filled the valley. "I'm sure some of them meant well, but I could never believe they cared for me as a person. I was afraid they only wanted physical contact with my body. I am attractive to men, I know, but that can be a curse. You are different." She stared into the turbulent water below them. "I tried to say this earlier, but could not find the words. You are the first man who made me comfortable."

"I don't get it. You're a gorgeous and desirable woman."

"There is a reason." Tears washed away further explanation.

He held her.

"Let's just enjoy the River Merse," she said, forcing back a sob.

Eventually, they went back to the car and found Cheri to thank her and let her know they were leaving.

"Come back again soon. By the way, I'm relieved you finally found a lady friend. I was beginning to worry about you."

"You and my cousins." He laughed.

Cheri walked over and gave Inga a hug. "And you come too."

As they drove out on the long, straight lane from the estate, Inga turned to face him. "I am happy you had not brought other girlfriends here. This will be our special place."

"Yes. Our special place." He nodded.

They drove for an hour before Cal turned at a sign for Rovine di Roselle. A few minutes later, he pulled into a gravel parking lot.

"From the marker, we must be at an archaeological site. Roman? Etruscan?" she asked.

"Both. The Etruscan is seventh century. The Romans built a town right on top of it five hundred years later. What's left is mostly Roman."

"This is a perfect spot for our picnic." She got out of the car and walked toward the ancient structures.

Cal put the two-euro fee in the lockbox, and they walked to a grassy knoll overlooking the ruins. It seemed to him that Inga's excitement replaced her melancholy from earlier. She knelt by the remains of a room floored by intricate mosaics and brushed away dirt. Time had reduced most of the walls to faint outlines connected by lines of crumbling bricks. Cal walked over to her and pointed toward a low wall on the other side of the stone road lined with deep grooves cut by chariot wheels. "That's the only Etruscan feature here in Rovine di Roselle, and it's barely visible beneath a younger Roman wall."

"I wish there were some Etruscan buildings. That was my favorite part of European history," she said, wiping sweat from her forehead, leaving a sienna smear.

He laughed and handed her a water bottle with a paper napkin from lunch. "You look the part of an archeologist, but you might want to wipe off the dirt before we get to town."

"Is it really that bad?" Pulling a mirror from her purse, she frowned. "Oh shit! Worse."

"Good. You're getting the hang of cursing in English. Once we get to Cerveteri, you'll receive your full Etruscan fix."

The drive from Roselle to Cerveteri was easy, but Cal knew the rest of the trip would be more challenging, because so many of the road signs were weathered and difficult to read. He handed her a map. "You navigate. We're going to a place called Banditaccia, a necropolis, literally a city of the dead. The tombs are domed structures and arranged along streets, like houses in a normal town, except they were houses for the dead."

"Sounds creepy. Is this going to be my Tuscan Gothic experience?"

"Possibly, but if you don't keep your eyes on the map, we'll never know. Didn't we just pass Via dei Fossi?"

"I am not sure." She squinted at the map.

"Okay. We just passed Via Maffia."

"I did not see it, and it is not anywhere on the map."

"Here's Via del Morro. Damn it! Do you see Via del Morro?"

He slammed on the brakes. When he turned to retrieve the map, her face was pressed against the window.

She slowly twisted around, offering him the map, accompanied by a withering glare. "Damn it, yourself. Maps are not my friends. Will I now be replaced by a GPS?"

Cal started laughing. "In the car, maybe, but never in bed. I knew getting to Banditaccia was a bitch, so I shouldn't have gotten so angry. I apologize. Are we still friends?"

"Of course, but I simply cannot read maps. Never could. None of my sisters can either; that was something my papa never understood."

"One of those gender things?"

"No, my mama is still very good. Better than Papa ever was, and it irritated him."

"Lucky a Rundstrom girl wasn't Leif Eriksson's navigator. He would never have discovered Vineland and beaten Columbus to the New World. Here, let me see the map. Okay, so we need to turn right on Via del Morro."

They backtracked and eventually drove into the Banditaccia parking area. Just like the other times he'd been there, it was empty. *If this were in the States, it would have been wall-to-wall cars*, he thought. The guard came over, and Cal gave him forty euros, twice the fee to get in. "Would you keep an eye on the car? Our luggage is in the trunk."

The man nodded and returned to his chair.

Cal slipped his camera in his pocket and took Inga's hand as they entered the city of the dead. "I wonder if he understood what I wanted."

"Hard to tell, but I cannot imagine any dead Etruscans will be interested in our luggage." She slowed and turned to take in the spectacle they were about to enter. "Are those grass-covered mounds the tombs? They look like misplaced igloos."

"Yes. They're called barrows."

They wandered down a dirt lane, lined on both sides with barrows. Most consisted of a stone wall five to ten feet high with an earthen dome covered by grass and shrubbery.

"Let's go into this one." She dropped his hand and ducked into the doorway nearest them.

He followed her through the entry corridor into a large central hall. Motion sensors activated electric lights, saving her from running headlong into a stone column.

"Slow down. We're a long way from a hospital."

She laughed and walked across the room. "Are these niches cut into stone for the remains of the dead?

"Yes."

"Lovely. I hope no one is home," she said, making a face.

"I'm sure we're very much alone. Everything has been sculpted into this soft volcanic tuff." He touched the wall as his eyes adjusted to the dim light.

She walked over to examine the next pillar. It was covered with pictures of swords, helmets, and eating utensils, all carved into the soft rock. "Are these objects the dead would need in the afterlife, like ancient Egyptian burial chambers?"

"Yes. This place is an elaborate cemetery for the Etruscan city Caere. The tombs date from the ninth to the third century BC." Cal warmed to the opportunity for an impromptu lecture. "The biggest of these circular barrows is nearly a hundred and fifty feet across. We've seen several good ones, but the best is ahead."

They continued down a winding path to a barrow nearly hidden under dense vegetation. The entrance passage was a trench cut into the overlying dome.

"They call this the Tomba dei Rilievi, Tomb of the Reliefs."

"But the sign says NO LIGHTS."

"Yes, and it will be pitch black." He grinned.

"We are not going in, are we?"

"You can't miss this." He pulled two small flashlights from his jacket. "Careful. It's damp."

She took a long step to a large stone nearly submerged in murky water. Her foot slid across the moss-covered surface. Cal jumped and caught her arm.

"I am so clumsy. Your shoes are soaked."

"Not as wet as you'd have been. But be careful. Don't want any broken bones."

They worked their way through the thick vines covering the massive doorway. The room ahead exhaled cool, musty air as Cal switched on his flashlight.

"Mind the floor; it's uneven and littered with rock," he said.

Twenty-five yards from the entrance, well beneath the top of the barrow, they entered a large room. The walls and columns were covered by images of animals, vases, daggers, shovels, and other domestic objects.

Cal pointed to the nearest column. "Here are the reliefs. See? They're not carved into the stone like in the other barrows but formed with stucco applied to the surface."

"And painted maroon and umber. It is so beautiful." Inga shone her flashlight on them. "I am glad we came. How old is Tomba dei Rilievi?"

"Relatively young—third-century BC, give or take a century." He took a few photos, and they moved out of the room into a cross passage.

"Which way?"

"As I recall, to the left."

"Can we get lost? The others were not this big."

"There aren't many passages. Try to remember whether we've gone left or right. Make a map in your head."

She sighed and gave him a look. "Did you forget I am the one who would have gotten Leif Eriksson lost?"

"Okay, I'll do a map for both of us and add it to your bill." After another twenty yards, they went into a small room. "Experts claim this is some of the best Etruscan art anywhere in Italy, but without bars or glass." They shone their lights over the paintings that covered the walls. "I'm happy you came with me." He pulled her close.

"So am I. This is special. Even better than the National Etruscan Museum in Rome, which I adore. I cannot believe we are standing here, surrounded by all this breathtaking art and not being watched by guards or security cameras. That couple"—she pointed to figures on the wall in front of them—"they are having sex. I feel like a voyeur."

"Look at the figures around the two Etruscan lovers. A two-thousand-year-old orgy. This is some of the most erotic art in the world. We shouldn't leave the lights on too long. Could damage the paint. Let me get a few more photos, and we'll be on our way."

They'd only gone a few feet before reaching another cross passage. She froze and looked wide-eyed at the darkness.

"What's the matter? We're not lost yet."

Fear had replaced excitement. Staring toward the room they'd left seconds earlier, Inga raised a finger to her lips. "Listen," she whispered.

He strained to hear the sound that seemed to terrify her. Voices. He heard them now, drifting out of the dark passage. He turned his light off.

She pushed Cal into a small recess, and they moved as far back as possible.

The voices grew louder, and after years in Austin, he couldn't fail to recognized their Texas accents. The newcomers carried lights that flickered across the wall near them as they talked about lunch. He was tempted to introduce himself, but he realized this would scare them of their wits; plus Inga seemed terrified by their presence. He stayed quiet and let them go past.

"Now! We must get out!" she breathed, stumbling into the inky blackness.

"Wait a second. We can't go anywhere without light." He switched on his flashlight.

"No!" Her body smothered the beam, causing them to stumble into the wall.

"What the hell is going on?"

"I know that voice. It is somebody from the lab. Someone who scares me."

"You can barely hear them now. They're gone and won't see our lights. I don't understand what you're afraid of, but let's move." He grabbed her hand, hauling her toward the entrance. They ran through the doorway, splashing carelessly out of the trench.

"Over here." Cal turned onto an overgrown path snaking to the top of the dome over the Tomba dei Rilievi. Panting, they looked down on the trail leading from the barrow they had left. The voices came again, barely audible above their own heavy breathing and the hum of insects.

"Down." She pulled him behind one of the thick shrubs covering the earthen dome. As the voices grew louder, they crawled forward to get a better look. Four people—a man, a woman, and two children—talked over each other, excited about what they'd seen and what they would tell people back home in San Antonio. Soon they headed down the path, back to the parking lot.

Inga stood up. Her body trembled as she put her hands on a large tree. In one violent convulsion, she lost everything she had eaten all day. Cal held her by the shoulders and gave her a handkerchief.

"Please forgive me. I'm so stupid." She blew her nose.

"What on earth frightened you?"

She laid her face against his chest. He felt the tears through his shirt.

"It's over. We'll talk about it later."

She gazed down the path after the now invisible family. "I have decided something. I am sorry I asked Mark to contact you. I do not want you to go with me."

He held her in front of him so only her toes touched the ground. "Maybe neither of us should go to your mysterious laboratory, but there is no way I'm *not* going with you if you feel you must return. So you might as well stop talking like that."

Her tears said all the thanks he needed. They climbed off the Tomba dei Rilievi burial mound and walked toward the entrance.

"I believe I've had enough of Banditaccia for one day. Let's let out of here and see if we can find a bottle of splendid Tuscan wine and talk more about what happened just now."

His hand felt a gentle squeeze, answering yes.

They drove back into the center of Cerveteri.

"How about there?" she asked, pointing to a trattoria down the street.

"Da Fiore is excellent. I ate there the first time I visited Banditaccia, but are you sure you want food?"

"Yes. I would like some food."

Cal parked, and they walked to Da Fiore.

A waiter met them at the door and led them to a table by the window. His *buonasera* was followed by a thirty-second monologue. He stopped and looked embarrassed. "From your expressions, I'd guess you don't speak Italian. Americans?"

"I am, but the lady is Swedish, and her Italian is no better than mine."

"Not a problem. My brother and I talk pretty good American."

"Let's start with a bottle of your best local red wine," Cal said.

"Here's a menu with translations. I'll be back quicker than you can say Jackie Robinson."

"Da Fiore was a good choice." He reached across the table and gently caressed her hands.

"Ah, *buonissimo*! It is *magnifico* when love survives into the winter," the waiter said as he returned with a bottle of Cerveteri Rosso. "An excellent little wine from our region, and not too many euros." He poured two glasses. "Have you decided on food?"

"Antipasto for now. We'll think about it a little more," Cal answered.

"*Perfecto!*" He waved and headed toward the kitchen.

"Did I get that right? When love survives into winter?"

"Yes, I am afraid so," she said.

"I suppose he meant it as a compliment, but I'd prefer it if we reminded him of summer or at least fall. Now tell me about this afternoon. What frightened you so badly?"

"The security man in our lab—the one from Texas. I thought it was him today."

"Why would he be here? And why would it scare you if he were?"

"I have seen him be very cruel. A month ago, he broke a bone in his foot. After that, he was like a wounded beast. If he knew I talked to you about the lab, I fear what he would do," she said with a grimace.

"Well, it wasn't him. I'm sure he's back in the lab terrifying the natives. Let's enjoy this delightful wine and gorge ourselves with Tuscan food. It will be the last for a while."

The waiter arrived with the antipasto. "Have you decided on what you'd like for dinner?"

"I have been reading about panzalella and torelloni. Shall we try it?" Inga asked.

"Let's."

"Don't rush your antipasto. I'll bring the panzalella and torelloni when you're ready. Would you like another bottle of wine?"

"It's excellent, but this will take care of us. We still have to drive to Rome."

The waiter nodded and returned to the kitchen.

She tasted the ham and salami. "Delicious. My appetite seems to have returned."

"Not surprised. Your stomach must be empty. We should eat so we can be on the road to Rome. Don't want to be too late getting to the hotel."

Shortly, the panzalella and torelloni arrived.

"Seems I was as hungry as you were," Cal said.

"I feel much better. Thank you. I will miss this Tuscan food."

It was close to midnight, and with the light traffic, the drive took less than an hour. Cal located their hotel near the SAS terminal at Leonardo da Vinci International Airport.

The roar of early morning flights woke Cal up. He reached over and gave Inga a nudge.

She rolled over with a groan. "You do not plan to drag me out to a cold patio again, do you?"

"No more cold patios, but we should be at the airport by eight o'clock."

After a quick breakfast, they were on the nine o'clock flight to Copenhagen. Cal's concern was growing by the hour about what awaited them in the laboratory they would were about to visit. He would find out soon enough.

They reached Kristianstad in the afternoon and turned their attention to the trip that would take them to Inga's mysterious laboratory.

Chapter 10

A Mysterious Island

They caught the 5:00 a.m. train to Copenhagen. Cal watched Inga continue staring out the window, and he wondered if he should ask her about the woman with white hair and when he'd learn the location of the secret lab other than that it lay somewhere in the Gulf of Mexico, near the Yucatán Peninsula. Within an hour, they were on an SAS flight to Mexico City.

The sun was beginning to lighten the eastern sky when the flight attendant brought two breakfast trays. "Would you like coffee?"

Cal nodded and glanced at Inga, who was too preoccupied with the passing clouds to care about coffee. "Two, please," he said.

The flight attendant smiled and disappeared into the galley and quickly returned.

"This might be good." He removed the plastic lid covering the tepid eggs.

Inga glanced at Cal and raised her eyebrows while moving her fork through the yellow mound on her tray.

"Not hungry?"

"Not especially." She blinked and turned away.

"You should eat something, even this. It may be a long day."

"I know. I will try."

From her peevish response, he knew this wasn't the best time to ask, but it had to be done, even if it should have been done much earlier. "Would a busty woman with short white hair mean anything to you?"

Leaning across the armrest, Inga frowned. "What did you say?"

"Do you know a woman with spiky white hair?"

"Was she pretty?"

"I wouldn't describe her as pretty, but there was something about her that's hard to explain. Sensuous in a tough-looking way, but I never saw her up close."

"Why would you ask about such a person?"

"I saw her sitting in a car near your apartment." From Inga's expression, it was clear this wasn't welcome news. "I also saw her in Lucca at the Torre Guinigi."

"Why didn't you tell me this before?" Inga shrieked, startling the stewardess, who nearly spilled their coffee.

"I'm sorry. I know I should have, but who is she?"

"The person you describe sounds like my cousin Aryanne Wolf. Her father was German. Papa didn't like the family at all. Thought they were dangerous, but the worst of all was her brother, Adolph. Apparently, he hated Sweden and our family in particular, so he was never around. I do not know what he looked like, but Papa said he had crazy eyes. Years ago, her uncle Markus was high up in the East German government. An officer in the state security service."

"The Stasi?"

"Yes, that is what they were called. Oh God, Cal. I thought she was gone from my life."

"Why would she be stalking you?"

"I wish I knew. She is mad, like her father and brother. I think she"—Inga choked, struggling for words—"wanted me to be her lover."

It was now Cal's turn to stir through the dregs remaining on his breakfast plate as he thought about this unwelcome intruder from Inga's past. He couldn't imagine what she might want from Inga, or even if she intended to harm Inga, but if this was her cousin Aryanne, it was not good. "She'll be in Sweden, and you'll be at your lab, so you won't need to worry about her for a while."

"You are probably right, but hearing about her is more disturbing than you can imagine."

"Back in Sweden, you can get a restraining order if she continues bothering you. But hell, Inga, we can't be sure if the woman I saw was your cousin or someone who looked like her."

Inga didn't respond and renewed her examination of the passing clouds while Cal stared with no interest at the tiny TV screen hanging in front of them. He desperately wanted to help her, and finishing this trip was only way to do that, but he realized much about Inga Rundstrom was still cloaked in mystery—possibly a dangerous mystery.

After landing and getting tickets to Mérida, they hurried to the twin-engine Cessna that was already boarding. "Looks like we can sit anywhere we like. They can't make money on this flight with just five passengers."

"I am sure they do not. Some people in the lab think the company subsidizes Mexicana to keep it running."

Cal leaned over and whispered, "I thought everyone would be speaking Spanish, but the other passengers are speaking German." Her response was a noncommittal shrug and a cautious grin he couldn't interpret. "Is the lab in Mérida?"

"No, it is just the nearest airport. We will take a taxi the rest of the way to Dzilam de Bravo. Not a long trip. Forty minutes, if the cab does not break down. A friend will meet us in there and take us to the island by boat."

Cal examined a map Inga had brought from the Mexicana counter. "Seems like we're headed for the middle of nowhere."

"Pretty close."

"Does it have a name?"

"I do not think so. Everyone just calls it 'the island.' It's not much more than a sandbank off the Yucatán coast."

"How big?"

"Several miles long, I would guess. A pile of sand a mile from shore."

"Sounds like a place not to be during a hurricane. Why couldn't you tell me this before?"

"As I said. They warned me not to speak about the lab. To be honest, I hated not telling you. All the secrecy now seems absurd."

The twin-prop Mexicana plane circled Mérida's small airport. After landing, it taxied past a sleek Learjet with RESTEMCO painted on its side. "That is the company plane," Inga said.

"Impressive. I know you mentioned the name, but what does *ReStemCo* stand for?"

"Research in Stem Cells. Someone told me they were going to call it StemCelRe, but it sounded too much like something from a spoiled salad." She smiled for the first time since leaving Copenhagen. "The rest of the trip is by taxi and boat."

They retrieved their bags from an unattended pile of luggage near the door and walked through the tiny terminal. Inga found a cab that looked like it might complete the trip to Dzilam de Bravo on the coast. "Here, let's take this one."

Cal studied the terrain as they approached Dzilam de Bravo. "I'll bet these woods are full of Mayan temples. Have you seen any?"

"Until I went to Sweden for Mama's birthday, I had not been off the island, but searching for Mayan temples would be fun."

Cal was relieved; she seemed to have left her funk about the insane cousin in Mexico City.

As the colorful buildings of Dzilam de Bravo came into view, Inga spoke to the driver in Spanish. The cab turned and stopped next to a long dock lined with small boats. She leaned out of the window and waved to a large man whose bushy black beard nearly hid his face.

"Hello, Theo. Good to see you," she said, jumping out of the taxi.

He came over and hugged her. "Dr. Cal Larsson, this is my friend Theoclymernus Papakonstandinou. Theo is the person who keeps us safe on the island."

The big man chuckled. "Yes, I chase away all the tourists and fishermen. Always good to meet a friend of Dr. Rundstrom," he said with a heavy accent. "You're not a tourist, are you, Dr. Larsson?"

"No, not a tourist; I'm here to help Dr. Rundstrom."

As Theoclymernus carried their bags to a powerboat at the far end of the dock, Cal whispered, "Seems like a pleasant sort, but aren't I supposed to be Eric Rosander?"

Inga smacked her forehead with the palm of her hand. "Oh, damn shit! How could I?"

"Pretty good," he said.

"What is good? That I am stupid?"

"No. Good to hear your Anglo cursing continues to improve, even if you did blow my cover." He laughed.

"Stop! This is not amusing. What do we do now?"

"Nothing that I can see except have a relaxing boat ride to your mysterious island. Do you really think it'll make any difference?"

"Things would be fine if I had actually brought a colleague who could help me with my work. Bringing an American geologist with no business being here might be trouble. Do you not remember what they said to me when I left for Sweden? Only people working in the lab are supposed to know this place exists and what goes on here."

"So how were your able to get permission to bring Rosander?"

"It was to the point where I needed help, and they let me choose someone."

"Let's hope Theo doesn't say anything."

The boat left the dock and skimmed over the tranquil blue water until palm trees appeared in the distance. As they got closer to the island, Cal saw a broad white beach and pastel buildings beyond it. "A tropical paradise, if appearances are any indication."

She didn't respond but squinted against the bright sun and bit her lip. Theo guided the boat past the jetty to a small pier. Cal jumped onto the dock, turning to pull Inga out of the boat. As they crossed the lush green lawn, he couldn't help but be impressed by the modern, obviously expensive buildings shaded beneath enormous palms.

"Nice. Pool, tennis, all the comforts of the wealthy," Cal observed.

"They do try to make things pleasant for us. Keeping people happy is hard out here, and ReStemCo does a good job. I hate the pool, but swimming in the Gulf is lovely. There are rooms with electronic games, billiard tables, and an especially big one for basketball. Everyone loves the bar, where everything is free, but I fear people drink too much. Let's go by your room first. Later, I'll show you around."

When Cal opened the door to his room, his bags were already there. From the outside, it resembled a Polynesian hut. He took Inga's hand, and they walked in. "Dr. Rosander finds this luxury suite wrapped in straw very acceptable."

"Dr. Rosander should be happy," Inga said. "They are usually reserved for the directors' visits. Mine is over there, near that palm grove. We are supposed to be professional colleagues, not lovers, so I had them put us in different cottages."

"Seems a little silly. Aren't we all adults?"

"I could get it changed, but I do not think we want to draw unnecessary attention to ourselves. Do you?"

"Perhaps not. Maybe I can sneak over after the housemother is in bed. Do you think they'll let me keep this room?"

"They might let Eric Rosander, not Cal Larsson. Sorry, but you must be off the island before Sunday when the directors return. I am afraid your limited knowledge of immunology would eventually become obvious."

"Who are the directors? They sound like fugitives from Orwell's *1984*."

"They are the company executives running the lab. Most speak German, like the men on our flight to Mérida. They are pretty invisible—except in the pool with the young girls brought from the mainland."

"Do you know where they're from?"

"My German is still pretty good from university, and I sometimes talk with them. I did hear several mention returning to Backer Villen, but I don't where it is."

"Never heard of it either. Maybe another of their labs."

Inga shrugged. "I do not know, but Chez ReStem closes at eight, and it is nearly seven. I will come back in half an hour."

"I gather Chez ReStem is where we eat."

"Yes. The food is excellent. I am sure you will agree." She turned and went to her cottage.

Cal took a Murphy's stout out of the refrigerator and sat on the porch. Aromatic camellia bushes, combined with lemony yellow flowers, added a powerful fragrance to the warm Gulf breeze. Combined, they created a powerful sleeping agent.

"Well, Dr. Rosander, are you enjoying your beer?" Inga asked.
"Until I dozed off."
"We should get over to Chez ReStem before they lock up."
"They wouldn't, would they?"
"They would!" She grabbed his hand. "Come!"

They walked into the large, well-appointed dining room, taking a table facing the beach, now lavender in the setting sun.

"Breathtaking," he said.

"In some ways, it is wonderful here, but I will be happy when I leave for good. I will get us something to drink from the bar. Another Murphy's for you?"

He nodded.

She walked away but was stopped by an Asian man with a small pencil mustache and ponytail. They chatted, and she continued toward the bar. Before she got there, another man who had just gotten a drink scuttled away toward the other side of the large room. The man reminded Cal of a diminutive Vincent van Gogh with his red hair and a pointed goatee. He joined a tall blond man whose unkempt beard was the ugliest Cal could remember. They moved into the shadows created by large potted plants, where they engaged in an animated exchange. Then they both left through a side door. It was as if they saw Inga but didn't want her to see them. Fascinated, Cal watched as the man he thought might be Chinese went over and looked out of the door. Trying to process what he'd just witnessed, he glanced back toward the bar as Inga returned with someone nearly as short as the redhead. His pallid complexion spoke of someone who hated the sun. He grabbed her arm as she reached the table.

"Dr. Rundstrom. Who's your new friend?"

"Dr. Frink, I'd like you to meet Dr. Eric Rosander. He is here to help me with our immunology problems. Eric, I'd like you to meet Dr. Carl Frink, our top medical technician."

Cal shook Frink's unresponsive hand. As he began speaking in Swedish, Inga held up her hands and laughed. "I'm sorry, Dr. Frink, but Eric is second-generation American and does not understand a word you are saying."

"My apologies. I thought you were Swedish. Nice to make your acquaintance anyway. Dr. Rundstrom, I'm glad you're back. We were wondering whether you've seen Dr. Goldman."

"No, but I got back just a few hours ago. Why do you ask?"

"No one has seen him for days. Just thought you might have run into him, that's all. Maybe he went fishing. I won't take any more of your time. Glad to meet you, Dr. Rosander. Good evening." Frink returned to a table near the bar, where he joined four other men wearing lab coats.

"What a smarmy character," Cal said. "I admit his pink Bermudas and matching lab coat are very Chez ReStem."

Inga wasn't smiling. "I cannot stand him, but that was an odd thing to say about Bernie. He hates fishing."

"Bernie?"

"Sorry. Bernard Goldman is a brilliant geneticist. He's one of the few people here I can talk to. Recently, he was threatening to return to UCLA. He had had enough of the lab. I prayed he would stay."

A waiter arrived with menus. "Can I get you a bottle of wine for dinner, Dr. Rundstrom?"

"That would be lovely. Let my friend chose." With a nod, Inga indicated Cal should answer.

"What are your reds?"

"Quite a fine selection, but if you like Pinot Noir, I'd recommend the Saint Galgano Guidotti 2005. Its nose is full, with a hint of layered flowers and nicely complex."

Cal turned toward Inga. "What's your favorite?"

"Whatever you choose. I like wine but cannot tell one from the other."

"Well, there it is. We'll try the Saint Galgano Guidotti."

The Pinot Noir arrived, and Cal pointed to the label. "Look. There's a rock with a sword sticking out of it on the label." She laughed out loud as he gently swirled the liquid, admiring the rich garnet color while savoring its aroma. He took another taste and swished it around in his mouth. "Excellent. First rate."

The waiter nodded and filled their glasses. "I'll return for your order in a few moments, madam."

Cal couldn't help but notice Inga's expression. "Oh, the wine connoisseur thing! I've been to enough tastings to figure out the game. That said, I don't have a clue what my nose and mouth are meant to experience, but it's fun, and it makes waiters go away happy."

When the waiter returned, Inga ordered chicken cordon bleu, and Cal ordered fried shrimp. After the waiter left, she said, "Everything's fresh. Someone goes to Dzilam de Bravo every day. The seafood comes straight off the fishing boats. It is quite fine. When I finally leave and have to cook again, my stomach may revolt."

"How much longer will you stay?"

"My contract ends on the last day in June. Then I will return to Kristianstad."

"Can we go to the lab after we eat? I'm curious to find out what's there."

"I checked the schedule earlier, and something's going on this evening. People will be around all night. Not a good time."

The food arrived. As promised, it was first rate. They finished and went outside.

"Let us take a walk. I need some fresh air," she said.

"The full moon is wonderful. Perfect night for a stroll on the beach."

They crossed the lawn, away from Chez ReStem's light. When they got to the shore, he reached down and ran his hand through the warm Gulf water.

"Nice! How about a dip? You swim naked in rivers, or so I've been told."

"I would love to, but now is when the sharks are most active. Several years ago, two people went for a midnight swim near here. One died; the other lost an arm."

"Enough said. What about during the day?"

"Never any trouble, I am aware of."

They left the beach and made their way to a sidewalk next to a row of dormitories but stopped at a sign warning DANGER—NO ACCESS BEYOND THIS POINT.

"The lab is over there," she said, pointing into the darkness.

"If you can't go beyond the sign, how do you get to the lab?"

"That warning is for staff, like cooks and waiters, not us, who work in the lab."

"What the devil?" Cal asked, motioning to a foot-high, miniature chain-link fence that bordered the sidewalk and separated the wild vegetation from the lawn. He walked over and nudged it with his foot. Then he bent down and touched it with one finger. "It's electrified, but not much of a kick. Why is it here? To keep rabbits from eating the lawn?"

"I do not think there are any rabbits on the island; at least I have not seen any. Do you usually check electric fences with your finger?"

"Only one finger at a time. That way, I will always have nine left." He guffawed. "This fence seems like lot of work with no purpose. I'm sure ReStemCo doesn't waste money on meaningless projects. Any idea why it's here?"

"None at all, but I have wondered about it. Anyway, it is a mystery we are not going to solve tonight, so let us go down and sit near the water."

They carried chairs from the lawn to the beach. Since leaving Chez ReStem, Inga's mood had changed from lighthearted to somber.

"Are you okay? Obviously, something's bothering you."

She continued looking at the moon's reflection in the peaceful water. "Cal, there is something I need to tell you." She stopped talking when two teenagers from the kitchen arrived to enjoy the evening and each other.

After they left, Cal turned and took Inga's hand. "You had something to tell me?"

"Not now." She got up and started walking toward her cottage.

Chapter 11

A Lilliputian Fence

Cal had heard the soft knock on the door but decided to ignore it. He frowned at the clock and then at the figure standing by his bed. "It's five o'clock," she said with a hint of amusement.

"I am aware of that." He sat up and reached out for her. "How did you get in?"

She laughed and backed out of his reach. "You did not lock your door."

"I didn't think this was a high-crime neighborhood."

She ignored his answer and pointed to the clock. "We must get to breakfast. I am in the lab at six thirty. Hurry and get dressed; you will need this." She held up an umbrella and opened the door. The edge that had crept into her voice startled him. Rain pelting the metal roof made a sound, compounding his feeling of unease. As they walked to Chez ReStem, she stared straight ahead.

"Last night, you were going to tell me something. What was it?" he asked.

She continued walking as if he hadn't spoken.

"Okay, but when do I get to see the lab? In case you've forgotten, that's why I'm here."

She continued to avoid eye contact. "After lunch. No one is scheduled then."

They finished breakfast in silence and went back to her cottage. "I'll be here at ten o'clock," she said with no further explanation.

"Okay, I'll amuse myself until then." He sat on the porch and watched her disappear into the downpour.

When the rain stopped, he went to his cabin for his camera. *Hell! Maybe I can find it myself and at least get a look. I have three hours.* He strolled down the beach to a point he thought was closest to the lab. He looked at the lush tropical vegetation and wished he had a machete or at least a large knife. After he stepped through a row of palms into the dense undergrowth, he tripped over a low fence like the one he'd touched the night before. "Oaf," he growled. He had just started walking again when a yellow two-story building came into view. *The lab*, he thought. Moving closer, he saw a man sitting on the roof. From his posture, Cal was sure he held a rifle. Staying hidden, Cal moved toward the building. Every twenty feet, signs written in several languages warned, TRESPASSERS WILL BE ARRESTED OR SHOT, and now he could see the man was Asian and cradled what looked like an AK-47.

Caution won over curiosity, and he found cover screening him from watchful eyes on the roof as he retraced his steps. He puzzled over what he'd just witnessed, when a metallic click made him jump. To his untrained ear, it sounded like a gun about to fire. He dropped to the ground and lay still. When nothing else happened, he crawled slowly in the direction of the noise. He saw a large cage sitting in a small clearing. A white mouse ran out of an open door; it was followed by another, until five rodents escaped and disappeared into the dense vegetation. Then the door clicked shut, making the sound he'd heard. *Curiouser and curiouser*, he thought. *This island is crazy as hell, and I haven't even seen the lab yet.*

He dashed back to the Lilliputian fence and jogged up the beach to his cottage.

After an unsuccessful nap, he went to her room. Inga arrived exactly at ten o'clock.

"Let's hike down the beach," she said as she grabbed two towels and took his hand. "I am sorry about being so bitchy earlier. It is a lovely day; maybe we can go for a short swim, if you are so inclined. We have two hours before I return to the lab."

"I know you have a lot on your mind. If we're going swimming, shouldn't we put on bathing suits?"

She laughed out loud and shrugged.

"Okay. I get it. Now is the time for me to shed my American inhibitions."

She led him down the beach, where he had been earlier. When they came to his footprints that disappeared into the undergrowth, he stopped. "You can get to a yellow building through there. Is it the lab?"

She wheeled around, dropping both towels. "Are those your footprints?"

"Yes. Dumb, wasn't it? I'm not supposed to be nosing around, am I?"

"No! What you did was not at all smart."

"We make piss-poor spies, don't we? First you blow my cover, and now this."

She was obviously irritated, but he continued. "I'm beginning to appreciate what goes on here."

"What do you mean?" She scowled as anger replaced annoyance.

"The kind of work you do in the lab."

Her expression continued to darken. "You did not sneak over there without me, did you?"

"No. It wasn't necessary. From out here, I could see the flying monkeys and hear the talking lions. Somehow, I missed the ruby slippers and munchkins."

"Damn it, Cal, this is real. None of what goes on here is funny."

He realized he'd crossed the line. "Okay. I'm sorry, but there was something else, and it's very real."

"What?"

"A large cage that automatically releases mice."

"Damn it, please be serious."

"I am—I swear. A little door opened, and some of them got out."

"Ridiculous! Why would someone do that? People try to catch mice, not free them."

"I know. This way." He took her arm, and after a moment's resistance, she followed.

They'd only gone ten feet, when Cal froze. "Inga, stop! Don't move." She had already seen the large snake lying in the weeds, nearly camouflaged by its tan and gray markings. It began to move and rise up, studying them. Apparently satisfied they were no threat, it began crawling away. In a moment of panic, Inga took a hurried step down the trail toward the beach, causing the large reptile to pause and rise again, imitating a snake charmer's cobra. It weaved back and forth in front of her.

"Easy," Cal said. "Don't budge. A snake's ability to see is based on motion. Don't move, and the bloody thing can't see you." They stood frozen, watching the snake, until it finally glided away from the trail into the bushes. "Must be a female. They're the big ones. She's almost seven feet long."

"I hate snakes," she said, sagging to her knees. "I am happy there are not so many in Sweden. Where did you learn so much about them?"

He went over and pulled her up. "In the book *Jurassic Park*. Well, it was actually a *T. rex* that could not see prey unless it moved. Seemed reasonable the same would apply to other reptiles."

"I'm glad I did not know the source for your information. I might have laughed, and the snake would have surely bitten me. Do you know what kind of snake it is?"

"A fer-de-lance. I nearly stepped on one during a birding trip in Guatemala. Nasty piece of work—one of the most poisonous snakes in Mexico."

"What is one doing here, so far from the mainland?" she asked.

He took her hand. "I have an idea, but let's leave before she comes back."

As they stepped onto the beach, Cal handed Inga a large palm frond. "Maybe we should cover our tracks." It didn't take them long to sweep away the telltale footprints.

"I remember hearing a story soon after I first arrived on the island.

Several years earlier, a group of young people from the kitchen crew were trying to find a place for a party away from the buildings, like the couple we saw last night. Three of them were bitten by a poisonous snake. One died. Could it have been a fer-de-lance, like the one today?"

"Very likely. They can be quite aggressive. I think the electrified fences are meant to keep them and the mice confined to the area around the lab. There must be just enough electricity to prevent them from wandering off. I think someone brought them here to be a deadly security force."

She shook her head in disbelief and looked back to where the snake had met them.

"Who is the guy I saw on the roof of the lab?"

"What did he look like?"

"Chinese, maybe—I couldn't tell for sure. One of the Greek's boys?"

"No. Theo makes sure no one accidentally comes here uninvited. His men are Mexican. His Spanish is excellent, and he trained them himself. And the snakes, I am sure he didn't bring them here. He and Bernie are good men, the only two on the island I trust."

"So, who is the green uniform on the roof?"

"A separate guard force, just for the lab, recruited from ReStemCo's Chinese plant. They only speak Chinese and are under the control of Simon Yeh. He's from Hong Kong—the only one on the island who can talk to them."

"I think I saw him in Chez ReStem last night. Good-looking guy with a thin little mustache and ponytail."

"Yes, and there is another person involved with security—Jack Archer, a tall Texan with long blond hair and a scraggly beard. I told you he's been in a terrible mood since he hurt his foot, just before I left for Sweden. Archer is the one I thought I heard in Banditaccia, the one who told me not to talk to anybody about the lab or the island. Theo and Simon do not like him. He left the island for a few days to be with the directors in the States and won't return until Monday."

Damn it to hell, Cal thought. *He's not in the States. He was with the little guy with red hair and a pointed goatee in Chez ReStem. I don't like this shit at all.* He was trying to decide what to tell Inga when she grabbed his hand

"Let's go back."

When they reached her cottage, she said, "Come in. I have something for you." She handed him a package. "Here, put on this white coat."

"I even get an official visitor's badge for Eric Rosander." He chuckled.

"You will need it to get inside."

Chapter 12

The Lab

At the door to the lab, she put her thumb on the scanner and slipped a plastic card into the slot. The heavy door slid open, and they stepped into a small room. A Chinese guard glanced up from his book. With a dip of his head, he nodded for them to pass after glancing at their badges. They went to the other side of the room, and Inga repeated the sequence to unlock a second door, which opened into a larger space.

As they walked in, she pulled Cal toward the wall and whispered, "When you take pictures, be sure the flash is off, and try to hide it. Security cameras watch all the time. I don't think the guard pays much attention to them, and your camera is small, but just be careful."

"For a super secret facility, security seems pretty lax. Looks like anyone could get in."

"I agree, but let us not complain. Hurry so we can get out."

In front of him were rows of shiny stainless steel boxes. Each had a thick glass window and was filled with greenish-blue fluid. As his eyes adjusted to the dim light, a luminous globular body emerged from the liquid. To him, the thing looked like a huge pink jellyfish stripped of its tentacles. Moving closer for a better view, he realized it was ever so slightly expanding and contracting—it was alive. He found the scene revolting and was about to turn away when he noticed a pulsing reddish mass near the thing's middle.

He stepped back and grabbed Inga by the arm. "What in God's name is this place?"

"Shh!" She held her finger to her mouth and whispered in his ear, "I told you this room is watched. Microphones and cameras." She glanced up toward the surveillance devices on the wall behind them. "You must be quiet and act like you are working."

He continued staring at the pink object floating in pale liquid. He turned toward Inga. "Are these the embryos?"

She nodded.

"They're huge. Four feet long."

"Yes. An enormous human embryo."

"I don't understand. How? Why? What are these boxes?"

"I cannot explain now. Take your pictures, and we'll talk outside. First I need to do some work." She took a clipboard and walked to another part of the room.

Doing his best to shield his camera, he filled a memory card.

Inga went to each box, examining the contents. She came over and spoke softly. "All right, I am done for now. Let us leave." She pulled him toward the exit.

As they went into the small outer room, the Chinese guard sat frozen as if Inga and Cal didn't exist. The door opened, and they left. Squinting in the bright sunlight, she took his hand and walked slowly to her cottage.

"If you had not seen it, would you have believed such a thing was possible?"

"Never. It's so damned eerie, who would believe it? What are these creatures, and what the hell are they for?"

"They're the reason for the lab's existence. To create large human embryos floating in these steel wombs. They begin with an embryo, just after fertilization."

"Where do they get them?"

"I'm not sure. There is a rumor that ReStemCo pays local girls to produce them."

"Prostitution with an evil twist."

She shrugged and unsuccessfully tried to smile. "When ReStemCo started this work, they discovered a way to allow the embryo to grow without forming specialized cells. It became no more complex than when growth began. Just a huge mass of embryonic stem cells. This seemed to accelerate growth. The thing went from one to thirty pounds in six months. In a year, four times larger. ReStemCo needs a great deal of material for their cell-based therapies. What they've accomplished is miraculous. Using replacement cells, they have therapies to treat Parkinson's and Alzheimer's, spinal cord injury, repair damaged heart muscles. But they had to have more than they could get with the standard methods. Everything went well, but then came the problems."

"What sorts of problems?"

"Some of the embryos began to mature, producing specialized cells, forming eyes, bones, arms, all the parts found in a fully developed human."

"I think I saw one near the door."

"I know. This surprised me. They are usually taken away from our lab. They are not at all useful for ReStemCo's purposes. One even grew hair. Many got sick. Something had gone wrong with their immune systems."

"Why?"

"ReStemCo did not know, but it needed to find a way to revitalize the immune system. That is why they brought me here. Another immunologist was here before I arrived, but she left. Disappeared without saying good-bye to anyone, and Bernie Goldman worried about the way she vanished."

"How about the maturation process? Is that solved?"

"No, it is evidently even more difficult than the weakened immune system. Bernie was concerned that the creatures could become fully developed, enormously large humans."

"Good Lord. They'd have giants from a netherworld?"

"Yes, but most of the people here pooh-poohed such an idea. They felt the bones and muscles would be so weak the creature could not function outside of the steel box. But Bernie told me he heard rumors that some did live and grew quite rapidly. He feared this might become

ReStemCo's new product. But if they are doing that, they would need larger boxes than we have on the island."

"Then ReStemCo could market an army of giants. If their brains could be controlled, they would do whatever their owners demanded. What happened to the ones that accidently developed into complete fetuses?"

"Every few months, a large helicopter landed near the lab. Our scientists were kept away until it left. After we went back, the most fully developed creatures were gone."

"Who took them?"

"No one knew, but the crew only spoke German, or that was the rumor."

"Inga, this is so fantastic, who would believe it? My camera has photographic proof, which could help us stop this insanity."

"That is why I wanted you to join me. To find a way to put an end to the lab and its disgusting research gone wrong." Her eyes glistened as she looked away.

"Well, we have our work cut us out for us, don't we?"

"Oh, Cal, I feel wretched that I brought you here. Your life may be in danger."

"Both of our lives, I'm afraid."

They walked onto the porch, and Inga sank into one of the wicker chairs.

"Does your cottage have anything to drink other than beer?" he asked.

"Pretty much anything you would like," she said.

He went inside and returned with two glasses. "This isn't Absolut. Is that okay?"

"It will be fine."

He turned on the radio and increased the volume. "Can't be sure these rooms aren't bugged like the lab, so we'll let them listen to music while we talk."

Inga didn't say a word but finished her drink.

"Another?" he asked. He went inside to get the bottle.

She took it and filled her glass again.

"Careful, or you're going to get pretty drunk," he said.

"What a good idea."

They sat quietly.

"Do you remember the morning in Kristianstad when I got so upset after you kissed me and tried to touch my breasts? And you asked me why I had never married?"

"Yes, of course."

"And if I would ever like to speak about it?"

"Do you want to tell me now?"

"I do," she whispered as she choked back a sob.

"Don't, if it's going to upset you."

She shook her head. "I must. It was thirty-six years ago; I had just turned fourteen. My parents planned a trip to Stockholm to buy a new car. They arranged for Kerstin, Ann, and me to stay with Aunt Edna and her husband, Yegor, for the weekend. The babies, Louise and Frederick, would stay with Papa's sister, Agnes. It was August, and every day seemed hotter than the one before it. We loved to visit Aunt Edna's lake house. In summer, swimming in the cool, fresh water was special, not salty and dirty like at the beach. Kerstin and Ann both got sick, so my parents decided to stay home and go to Stockholm later. I put up such a terrible fight, Mama gave in. I would spend the weekend there with no sisters. A dream come true. After breakfast, Aunt Edna and Yegor arranged to visit friends who lived across the lake. They asked me if I wanted to go. Naturally, I said no. Would a young girl want to sit around with old people on a beautiful Sunday afternoon? I promised to stay out of the water until they returned in a few hours. After they left, I went down and sat on the dock in a little cove you would not notice unless you were in a boat right at the entrance. The sun was warm, so I took off my clothes and lay down. Something moved in the bushes near Yegor's shed, the one he used as a workshop in the winter. When I looked again, I did not see anything. After a few minutes, I dove into the lake and swam to shore. As I got out of the water, Yegor stood staring at me in a way no man had ever done before. It was awful. I can never forget how he grabbed my arms. I could not scream. He dragged me into the shed and began touching me. I cried, but he would not stop. Then he ... he ..."

"He raped you."

"Yes." Her soft whimper turned into violent sobs. "That horrible man raped me."

"Oh, Inga, I'm so sorry." He knelt in front of her and held her. She rocked gently back and forth, gulping air between sobs.

"Three months later, they found I was pregnant. At first, my parents did not believe the story. Only Ann, who was thirteen, believed me. She had also seen Yegor's look. At Aunt Agnes's Christmas party, Yegor got quite drunk. He began bragging about how he had sex with the pretty little thing he caught as she walked naked out of the lake near his dock. Papa heard this and grabbed Yegor's arm. 'Was that Inga ... my Inga you raped last summer?' He was too drunk or too stupid to deny it. Before Papa could reach him, an older cousin, Aryanne, jumped on Yegor. She stabbed him with a small knife. It took several men to pull her away. So horrible—blood and cursing—chairs knocked over and broken. Seems as if happened yesterday."

"She is the woman with white hair who followed you, isn't she?"

"Yes."

"What became of Yegor?"

"No one saw him again after the party. We thought he may have returned to Russia. Poor Aunt Edna's heart broke when she heard the story of my rape and then his disappearance. She died a year later. Too much drink, my parents said. There is one other thing."

"What?"

"A week after the dreadful Christmas party, I received a note telling me I would never have to worry about Yegor again."

"Who wrote it?"

"There was no signature, but I recognized the handwriting."

"Someone you knew?"

"Aryanne, I'm sure."

"Did she kill him?"

"I have no evidence, but I think so."

"What happened to the baby?"

"I miscarried a month after the party."

"Inga, you've been through enough this evening. Please stop."

"No! I never told anyone about this before, and I want to finish. After that August, I hated men. Boys would ask me to go out. I treated them badly. I am sure people wondered, because I was not ugly. Some said I was pretty. I was not attracted to girls, but men terrified me. I was nearly through college before I finally went on a date. When the poor man tried to kiss me, I slapped him. So you see, Cal, that is why I never got married or had a lover."

He put his arms around her and gave her a tender kiss. "Thank you for feeling comfortable enough with me to open up like this."

"Tonight was an exorcism for me. I feel better."

"Good."

They sat on the porch, enjoying a final drink.

"Don't go." She led him into her cottage, closed the door, and switched off the light.

The gas lamps surrounding the lawn filled the room with a soft glow, enough to see her blouse had slipped off her shoulders, joining the skirt on the floor. They went into the bedroom, and she pulled him onto the bed.

They slept soundly, until Cal was awakened by a noise. He got up and walked to the porch.

Rubbing her eyes, she joined him. "What is the matter?"

"Thought I heard something." They stood looking into the dark. "There it is again, and not far away."

She nodded. He recognized the fear in her eyes he'd seen in the Tomb of the Reliefs. A harsh voice with a Texas accent bellowed obscenities about getting that Swedish bitch.

"I don't understand. Why is Archer back now? He went with the directors to the States and should not have returned yet!" she cried.

"I'm afraid it is Archer. I think I saw him in Chez ReStem the first night we arrived."

Her expression of shock and horror stunned Cal. "I need to go to my room. We've got to leave this island if we can. I'll be back in a second."

CHAPTER 13

A Note on the Floor

The full moon made lights along the path unnecessary as he went to get the few things he'd take. He wasn't sure where they'd go, but they couldn't stay where they were. He was nearly there when he saw movement out of the corner of his eye—a shadow running away from his cottage. He started to give chase but realized there was no time. He pushed the door open and reached in for the light switch. Nothing seemed out of place except for a piece of paper lying on the floor. He turned on a lamp and read it.

> Dr. Larsson, you and Dr. Rundstrom are in great danger. They know you are not who you claimed to be and plan to act tonight. Leave as soon as possible. These are dangerous men. There will be a boat near the beach west of the jetty. The mainland is a mile to the south. Good luck, amigo.

Cal grabbed his passport, his wallet, and the memory card with the photographs from the lab. He dashed back along the path to Inga's cottage and shoved the door. It opened with an unintentional bang. "There's not a minute to spare. Let's go."

"Where are we going?" she asked.

"Don't talk! There's no time. Hurry! We're in real danger. This note was on the floor when I got to the room."

She snatched the crumpled paper out of his hand. "Who sent it?"

"I have no idea, but we'd better take it seriously after the voices on the lawn. Bring only what you need. No clothes."

She opened her suitcase, frowned, and grabbed her purse.

"Quick!" He pulled her along the path leading away from the villas. From behind the building to their right, they heard excited voices of people speaking Chinese. Cal and Inga raced across the broad lawn toward the beach and the waiting boat.

"Stop or you will be shot!" Both recognized the Texas accent. Seconds later, gunshots pushed them to run faster.

"Keep going," Cal called to her. "With Archer's bum foot, he won't be able to keep up with us."

For a hundred yards, the shadows from giant hibiscus gave them cover, but now they were near the beach. The boat that had carried them from Dzilam de Bravo bobbed in the shallows, a few feet from shore. He held her hand tightly as they ran step for step. The shooting started again. Bullets whined over their heads and thudded into the sand.

"Damn you, Simon. Your men aren't trying to hit them." Archer stopped and steadied himself, taking careful aim.

Cal felt her hand slip away as she fell without a sound. An instant later, a searing pain exploded in his leg. He went down, striking his head on the packed sand. The last thing he remembered was a wave washing over his body.

"Can you hear me?" a disembodied voice asked. Cal no longer lay on the beach, but the throbbing in his head made focusing on the speaker difficult. "Dr. Larsson, can you hear me?" the voice asked again.

"Yes." He forced himself to speak.

"How do you feel, Dr. Larsson?"

"Like bloody hell. How do you think? Where am I?"

"In ReStemCo's clinic. The bullet went through your left leg but didn't hit any bones or do serious damage. You will be walking soon. Your head took a nasty knock, but no concussion."

As Cal's mind cleared, he recognized Theo; the events of the previous night returned with horrifying clarity. "Where's Inga? Is she okay?"

Theo remained silent, eyes fixed on the floor. He looked up, imperceptibly shaking his head.

"God damn it, answer me! Where's Inga? If you won't help me, I'll find her myself." When his left foot hit the floor, he collapsed.

"Stop, please. I'll take you to her." He motioned toward the door, and one of his men arrived with a wheelchair. Theo pushed him down the hall, stopping in front of a closed door. "Dr. Larsson, I want to prepare you—"

Before he could finish, Cal wheeled himself into the small poorly lit room.

"Inga," he whispered as he moved toward the table where she lay and pulled down the sheet that covered her. He knew she was dead from the moment he walked into the room. Now he saw the gruesome hole in her forehead and slumped next to her body.

"The bullet entered the back of the skull and exited through the front of her head," Theo said.

His clinical description of the wound left Cal numb. "You murdering son of a bitch. Why did you kill her?"

"Please believe me, my men and I did not do this. She was a good friend." He put a hand on Cal's shoulder. "I'm afraid you don't understand what sort of people run this place."

"That's some shit, pal, and you're one of them!" His tears transformed the little room into a white haze; he couldn't continue.

"No, I am not one of them. If I were, you would be dead by now."

Cal held her cold hand and kissed it. "Damn. Why did it end like this?"

Several days passed, and the memory of their fatal dash across the beach replayed over and over in Cal's mind. Sleep that never lasted long brought him back to the small room with Inga's lifeless body.

Theo's guards brought meals, which Cal ignored. Heavy bars on the windows and a steel door showed this hospital room doubled as a prison cell. He was not going to get out by himself. On the third day, after the guard removed the day's uneaten food, Cal saw Theo standing in the doorway.

"Are you feeling better, my friend?" asked Theo.

"You're no damned friend of mine." Cal's eyes locked on the man looking back at him.

"I understand, but we need to talk," Theo said quietly. "Let's go outside. These walls have ears." Cal shunned the wheelchair and hobbled out to join the Greek behind a thick hedge that hid them from anyone in the building. "I realize you won't believe me, Dr. Larsson, but I'm sorrier than you can ever imagine about Dr. Rundstrom. My heart aches, amigo."

Cal's head jerked up. "You're the one who left the note in my cottage, aren't you?"

"Yes. A week ago, most of the staff went to a meeting in the States. They are scheduled to return tomorrow. For some reason, Archer came back early. He was suspicious, had your room searched, and discovered your passport showing you were Cal Larsson, not Eric Rosander."

"You understood from the beginning, didn't you?"

"Yes. As you remember, Dr. Rundstrom introduced you the day we met on the dock in Dzilam de Bravo."

"Why did Archer come after us like that?"

"The day she died, I saw a message on his desk directing him to 'take care of her that night.'"

"Are you telling me whoever wrote it intended for him to kill Inga?"

"Yes, I'm sure of it. That's why I warned you."

"Who sent it?"

"Only the name Adolph was on the note. I've seen it before but never met this person. All I know is he is the one who gives Archer instructions."

"Why did he want Inga dead?"

"Why would anyone want such a thing? But I think they were afraid she might tell others what goes on here. I listened to Archer talking once, and ReStemCo worries what would happen if the public discovered how they produce embryonic stem cells on an industrial scale and how that might affect the market for their therapies."

"But enough to commit murder?"

Theo shrugged and raised his massive eyebrows. "ReStemCo's stockholders could lose a fortune. Many powerful people are heavily invested in the lab."

"Security is your department. Why did you let this happen?"

"Dr. Larsson, I've told you before, my job is to keep fishermen and tourists from landing here. When I got the position with ReStemCo, I never imagined anyone might be killed just for coming here. The night when you ran toward the boat, Simon told his men to shoot high or into the sand but not to hit you."

"How do you know? He only speaks to them in Chinese."

"He told me later, and he also kept Archer from killing you on the beach. Simon was angry; he said he wasn't hired to be a cold-blooded murderer."

"Do you believe Simon's story?"

"Yes. He and Archer hate each other. My men guarded your cell to keep Archer from completing what he didn't finish on the beach that night."

"The way they use those creatures in the lab as factories to produce embryonic stem cells is wrong. Inga thought they felt pain—it needs to be stopped. I'm sure that's what she wanted."

"I don't know much about what happens in the lab, but I think she was right. It's horrible what happened." Theo shook his head. "You must leave tonight."

"How?" Cal asked.

"I'll see that the door is left unlocked. The boat will still be near the jetty after ten o'clock. Go to the mainland, and catch a plane to somewhere safe, anywhere other than your country. A large net will be spread to find you. You know something many powerful people want kept secret, and there's only one way they can be sure of your silence."

"I'll need money and my passport. They were with me on the beach. Can you get them?"

"They're locked in a safe, but I know the combination. When your dinner arrives, look in your shaving kit."

The guard who brought his food that evening said something in Spanish and produced the maroon shaving kit. As Theo had promised, the wallet and the memory card were inside.

When a clock in a distant office struck ten, he opened the door and slipped into the cool night. The bullet wound slowed him, but he reached the beach in fifteen minutes. The boat was still there. Memories swept over him like an emotional tsunami. Now standing a few feet from safety, tears filled his eyes. *Damn!* he thought. *Why couldn't it have been like this three days ago? Theo had done a good job.* The fifty-horsepower Johnson came to life on the first try. This wasn't a particularly noisy motor, but it sounded like a Boeing 707 to Cal as he eased the boat forward. Once past the jetty, he went full throttle toward the mainland.

From inside Chez ReStem, the young bartender watched Archer lounging on the patio as the Texan finished half a fifth of bourbon. His job was to keep a full glass of ice and a bowl of snacks on the table. In five years as a bartender, he'd never seen anyone so rude and vulgar. Ever since the killing, he'd gotten worse, like a man possessed.

With three of his Chinese guards, Simon approached Archer, who was so drunk he didn't notice until he saw the muzzle of a rifle inches from his head. Through an alcoholic haze, he glared at the rifle and then Simon as his hand came to rest on the nine-millimeter Glock in his holster.

"Don't be stupid, Archer. Slowly lift it up and put it on the table. We'll need it for forensic evidence."

"Forensic evidence. What the hell for?" Archer snarled.

"For the murder of Dr. Rundstrom. But why did you do it?"

"I had to kill her. She couldn't leave the island."

"If you wanted to stop her from leaving the island, my men could have sunk the boat, and nobody would have been hurt."

"You don't understand. She had to die."

"I'll ask again. Why?"

"I had my orders. She had to die."

"You're one sick son of a bitch. Get up. My men will take you to your room. You'll stay there until the directors return."

As they started to leave, the noise of the motorboat's engine drifted across the patio.

"Must be some late-night fishing, but Theo will take care of it." Simon glared into the darkness and gave Archer a push.

Cal cruised along the shore until the lights of Dzilam de Bravo glowed in the distance. He slowed down and looked for a safe place to land. He had to be careful. Even though it seemed unlikely the alarm had been raised yet, an American landing at night near a small village on the Yucatán Peninsula would surely interest the local police.

After a few minutes, Cal pulled up next to a small dock near a house whose windows were dark. He climbed out of the boat to look for a large rock and glanced back at the house, hoping the owners weren't home, because this was going to be noisy. It didn't take long to knock a hole in the floor of the boat. He sat on the dock, gave a kick, and watched it drift into deep water and sink. He approached the house as a dog began barking. Cal was relieved when he saw that it was inside. He froze and waited in the shadows. When no one came out of the house, he walked to the road leading to the glow of Dzilam de Bravo.

It was Saturday evening, and the streets of Dzilam de Bravo were full of noisy crowds. Cal found a hotel on the edge of town. He desperately wanted to get away from this place, but according to the bus schedule in the lobby, leaving would have to wait until morning. He'd fly from Mérida to Mexico City. He wasn't sure what would happen next. Someplace safe, Theo had said, but not home—not to the United States because that would be where they'd start looking. So where? Tomorrow, after a night's rest, maybe he could decide.

Sunlight pouring through the open window and loud voices on the street below woke him with a start. He walked over and watched as three uniformed policemen shouted at a short, balding black man, who Cal recognized as the hotel clerk from night before. The only word he caught was ReStemCo, but that was all he needed to hear. He dressed and, with his only luggage the maroon shaving bag, headed toward the rear of the building. The police continued haranguing the clerk, so Cal limped down a dark stairway into a deserted alley at the rear of the hotel.

If the authorities were looking for him, the bus station would be too risky, so he found a taxi and explained that he wanted a ride to Mérida. The driver opened the door and nodded for Cal to get in. He dozed until the cab came to an abrupt stop. In front of them, cars were being searched by heavily armed policemen.

"Here, get on the floor, and pull this over you." The driver tossed a filthy blanket over the seat.

"You speak English?"

"What do you take me for—an ignorant Mexican who speaks only one language? I worked in your country for five years. In North Carolina, cutting lawns. Have you heard of this place?"

"As a matter of fact, that's where I live. Why are they stopping cars?"

"I heard earlier this morning, the police are looking for a gringo with a beard. They say he murdered a woman on an island. Shot her in the head."

"Weren't you afraid to let me in your cab? I might be the man they're after."

"I'm sure you are the one they're looking for, but I don't think you murdered anyone. I know faces. Yours is not a killer's face. Am I right?" he asked.

"You're right. My friend was shot, but not by me."

"I told you, I know faces. Stay on the floor; we're almost there."

Cal knew enough Spanish to understand as the cabbie explained that he was on his way to Mérida to pick up his mother-in-law and would be happy if they'd make him go back to Dzilam de Bravo. Laughing, they slapped him on the back and told him to continue on to his mother-in-law's.

"Get up now. You're safe, my friend with the bad reputation."

Cal squeezed the man's shoulder. "I'm glad you came home."

They both laughed.

Cal closed his eyes when the image of his first meal in Chez ReStem flashed across his mind. *The little guy with the red goatee had been in a very animated conversation with Archer, the tall blond man with the terrible beard. It wasn't long until he shot Inga. Was the man with red goatee involved in Inga's murder?* Cal wondered. *Was he the mysterious Adolph?*

When they reached the airport, Cal got out and handed the cabbie two crisp new hundred-dollar bills. "I owe you a great deal. I can't thank you enough," he said.

"You thank me more than I deserve. Have a safe trip to wherever you're going."

Cal headed toward the Mexicana counter. No one paid any attention to him as he purchased a one-way ticket to Mexico City. His flight wouldn't leave for three hours, so he had time for breakfast. Next, he visited a luggage shop. Even if the police here weren't looking for him, an American passenger with no baggage might be viewed as someone worth talking to. He filled the small suitcase with underwear, socks, a shirt, pants, and his maroon shaving kit. Now he looked more like a tourist; one who packed light. In the barbershop at the far end of the tiny concourse, he lost the beard he'd worn for thirty years and had his hair dyed. He hardly recognized the person staring at him from the mirror, except for wrinkles and the sad eyes. For now, that was a good thing.

The flight to Mexico City took two hours. It was then that Cal decided where his safe place would be. He located the British Airways counter, purchased a ticket to Ireland, and waited in the far corner of the boarding area.

Chapter 14

✵

Hello, Kara O'Malley

Cal relaxed the moment the big plane left Mexico City, but no sooner were his eyes closed, he was on the beach where Inga was shot—then in the little room with her body.

A hand lightly touched his arm. "Sir, would you like something to drink? We'll be eating in an hour," the attendant asked.

He shook his head and closed his eyes again.

The sound of wheels being lowered brought him out of a deep sleep. The plane had begun its descent to Shannon. He cleared customs, located an ATM, withdrew five hundred euros, and found a bus bound for Galway. During the ride, he enjoyed the lush green countryside, so different from Dzilam de Bravo's burnt landscape.

When the bus pulled into the terminal, Cal realized he didn't remember Kara's address. Fear of the unknown was pulling with both hands to turn him around and go anywhere but here. He pushed back. Leaving now without seeing her was a mistake he wouldn't make. After retrieving his small suitcase, he went into the Imperial Hotel.

"Could I get a room for the night?"

The desk clerk opened the reservation book. "Certainly. Would you prefer smoking or nonsmoking?"

"Non, but I'll wait a bit. I didn't realize you allowed smoking."

"We don't. That was a question I asked for so many years; I guess old habits die hard." He chuckled and looked into his reservation book. "A room will be available when you're ready."

"One more thing. Could I look at your Galway phone directory?"

He thumbed through the well-worn pages. "O'Malley ... Donald ... James ... Kara. There it is, 221B Cook Street."

It was a short cab ride, but long enough to remind him how much he liked Galway. He could imagine living here.

Cal paid the driver and walked toward the house. He stood for a moment, looking at the immaculate yard. As he opened the gate, a large man walked around the corner of the house.

"Not selling something, are you, lad?" He stopped short and squinted. "By God! Calvin, is this you, come from the States? I didn't recognize you. How are you?"

"Good, and you, Mike?" To Cal's relief, Mike's handshake was friendly, if painfully firm.

"I'm fine. Didn't know my little sister was expecting a visit, but she never tells me anything."

"Actually, she wasn't, but she seems to be keeping you busy."

"You don't know the half of it, Calvin, but look at the yard. A thing of beauty." He grinned.

The screen door shut with a bang. A woman with long auburn hair flew across the yard, surprising Cal with a passionate kiss. "Larsson. I would recognize your mug, with or without a beard."

Kara's face and expressive green eyes reminded him how smitten he had been the first time he saw her in the grad students' lounge at Texas, where she was an instant favorite with the male teaching assistants. He relished the closeness of her body, but as Inga's memory returned, he gently pushed her away.

"Larsson, is something wrong?" Her furrowed brow revealed the confusion caused by his unintentional rebuff. "Let's not stand out here all day. I'll fix drinks. Come on, Mike."

"Some other time. I'm not finished with the lawn, and you two have a lot to talk about. I'll be by tomorrow. Calvin and I will negotiate how he'll finally take you off our hands."

"Thanks, Michael. You're hilarious." She turned and went back into the house.

"I'll do what I can." Cal winced as the image of Inga's lifeless body smothered the playfulness of the moment. In Iceland, he'd resolved to visit Ireland and jump-start his romance with this Irish woman he never completely stopped loving. But that was before Inga, and being here wasn't fair to Kara.

He followed her into the house. "I'm happy to see you, Larsson, but you might have given me a little warning. Would you like tea or coffee?"

"Coffee would be great."

"How are you, and what brings you to Ireland?"

"I'm good. Why I'm in Ireland is a long story."

"I had a feeling it might be." She smiled. "Tell me about it later, but now I want to hear about North Carolina and your family."

"All fine. Brenda finally finished her degree. Graduates in less than two weeks."

"Did you bring pictures of her daughters?"

"No. Sorry."

"Shame on you."

"She gets on me for that too."

Mike hollered through the screen door, "The lawn is done, but I never got any tea!"

"Give me a second, and I'll heat the water."

"Only teasing, love. I should be getting home. Clair will be wondering what new projects you've invented for me. Good to see you again, Calvin. I'll try to come by tomorrow so we can catch up." He left, giving Cal a thumbs-up.

"It is lovely to see you, Cal, but it's been so long. How are you?"

"I'm good. Retired a month ago."

"That's wonderful. Knowing you, I'm sure you're keeping busy," she said.

"I'm working on it. And how about you?"

"Still in the environmental geology business. Mostly pollution from the farms and small manufacturing companies around Galway. You know the drill. People screw up the water they drink and expect someone else to fix it."

"No shortage of jobs, then." He sipped his coffee and enjoyed the view over the edge of his cup. Shorts and tank top revealed a well-preserved figure little changed since they were in Texas.

"Can we talk about e-mails? Since I didn't hear from you, I feared the EU terminated communication between Ireland and North Carolina," he said.

She stared through the window like she'd never seen the trees in her backyard before. "I'm sorry, but I stay so busy and never quite knew what to write, but I did miss you."

"I missed you too, and we need to talk," he said, patting her hand.

"Especially why you pushed me away there in the front yard when I kissed you. There is more to this visit than simply coming by to say hello, isn't there? You arrive out of the blue with no warning. And your face—I've never seen you without a beard, and since when did you start coloring your hair?"

"I didn't do it because of vanity, but to stay alive."

Kara stood up and got a bottle of Jameson. She poured two glasses, and they sat on the couch.

"Tell me."

"I thought you found someone else when I didn't hear from you," Cal said. "Then, a few weeks ago, I got a phone call from Mark Svendson. You remember him, don't you?"

"Yes, of course."

"He said a friend in Sweden had a problem and thought I could help. I already had plane tickets to visit my cousins, so I thought I'd meet her and see what I could do."

"Is the 'she' with a problem pretty?"

"Yes, quite. I went with her to the laboratory where she worked. They do off-the-wall research like creating gigantic embryos for stem-cell therapies."

"Jesus, Larsson, that's light-years beyond off the wall. What does she want you to do?"

"At first, she said she wanted advice, but really she wanted me to help her stop what they were doing."

"Did you?"

"No. Before we were able do anything, she was killed. Murdered."

"Larsson, I'm so sorry. What was her name?"

"Inga Rundstrom."

"Were you close?"

He examined his glass of Irish whiskey. "I stayed with her in Sweden while I tried to learn enough about immunology to bluff my way into the lab where they create the giant embryos."

"You've lost me. Why didn't you just go?"

"The company is super secretive and doesn't appreciate uninvited guests. She couldn't return right away, so we took a trip to Tuscany."

"Sounds like you two became close." Her eyes narrowed.

"No denying it."

"Were you lovers?"

"If you're asking if we had sex, the answer is yes."

"Did you love her?"

"Yes, but before I met her, I'd decided I would come to Ireland. Just wanted to try one more time to see if we could make our relationship permanent."

"Then you met Inga, and you knew she must be the one."

"Yes, something like that. She seemed perfect, but I couldn't shake the nagging fear I'd never be free of the Irish girl."

She stared down into her glass as a tear feel into the golden liquid. "See what you made me do? I never cry, but now the damned tears are ruining my Jameson. I wish I'd answered your first e-mail and told you how much I was still in love. I guess some things are meant to be, and some aren't." She gave him a hesitant smile and took a long drink. "Larsson, you've told me one hell of a story. Is there any proof about the lab?"

"Yes, but first, I want to do something. Could I use your computer and printer?"

"Sure; my office is this way."

"Give me an hour, and I'll explain."

When he returned from her office, he put a pile of photos on the coffee table.

She looked at them and winced. "Those creatures are dreadful. Tell me everything."

As he finished the story about Inga, the island, and the steel wombs, the clock struck the hour. "Is it really three in the morning?" he asked.

"I'm afraid so." She looked at the nearly empty Jameson bottle and smiled. "If you hadn't been the one who told me this, I'd never have believed a word of it. What now? Seems like you've made a few dangerous enemies on this trip."

"In Mexico City, I thought there was only one place to go, so here I am. Now, I realize that was selfish. They'll easily track me to Ireland, maybe even to Galway. My being here will be dangerous for you. I should go to the hotel right now and leave Ireland altogether."

Kara slid closer. "Possibly you've forgotten, love, I own one hell of a bad Irish temper. Unless you'd like to find out how bad, don't say rubbish like that again."

"Kara," he said.

Her finger touched his lips. "Please shut up. This is settled; you stay here. Are you hungry?"

"Hadn't thought much about food, but a little something would be good. Isn't there an all-night pub nearby?"

"In case you missed it, we killed a whole bottle of whiskey. I don't fancy wrapping my car around a tree. Let's be satisfied with what's in my fridge."

Cal stood up, surprised how the room shifted under his feet.

Kara pulled a chair toward him. "Here, sit." Like magic, the small kitchen table was covered by cold ham, cheese, bread, hard-boiled eggs, and jam. "I'll make some tea."

He was too busy reconciling food with the revolving room to argue.

They ate in silence until she finally asked, "What are you going to do next?"

"Get some sleep, I suppose."

"Didn't mean *that* next. What are your plans for those photos? From what you've told me, the people from the lab might arrange for a deadly accident."

"Possibly, and that's exactly the reason I shouldn't be here. I can't risk anything happening to you too."

"Damn it, Larsson, we've already settled this. You're not just another chum from university. You're staying here until we sort things out. Tomorrow we'll start. There's a comfortable bed in the room with the computer."

"Soon I'll have collected enough material for a short story about computers as substitute lovers," he muttered with a self-deprecating chuckle.

"I'm meeting a client tomorrow at nine. Will you be okay?"

"I'll be fine, but before you leave, I have a favor to ask."

"Ask away."

"Didn't you have a friend in the Foreign Office?"

"Yes, Judy Lindsey, in the security section. I've known her forever."

"Would you ask her to check if she can find any recent newspaper articles that might relate to the island, especially about Americans in the Yucatan Peninsula area?"

"I'll call in the morning, before I leave."

"Thanks," Cal said, joining her computer for the night.

The next morning, Kara smiled as he entered the kitchen. "You look like hell, Larsson."

"No worse than I feel. How about you?"

"Fine. It's the Irish gene. We know how to handle good whiskey. Sit and eat breakfast. You'll probably survive," she said, handing him a steaming cup of coffee.

He sat and gingerly massaged his head. "Kara, you're a saint."

"Bite your tongue. That's one accusation I wouldn't want to get around."

She stuffed several folders into a well-worn briefcase he recognized from their days at Texas and waved as she left. "Back by noon."

Cal walked the half mile to Abbeygate Street. He bought himself some clothes and then spied a leather goods store.

"May I help you?" asked the clerk.

"I'm looking for a briefcase. Something that can carry a big load."

"For you?"

"A lady friend."

"How about this one? Fine Italian, and reduced to one hundred euros."

"Perfect! Exactly what I was looking for. Will you gift wrap it?"

He paid cash. He didn't think the directors from the lab could trace credit card transactions, but caution seemed advisable.

The woman chatted as she boxed and wrapped the gift. He picked up the package and headed for the door.

"Good-bye, love," she said with what he fancied was a seductive smile.

He walked down the street with no particular destination in mind. From the Salmon Weir Bridge, he went to the Cathedral of Saint Nicholas and the Assumption. He'd always been fascinated by cathedrals—Gothic, Romanesque, Catholic, Lutheran, or Anglican. He loved the scale and architecture, especially this one with its green copper roof, domed tower, and stone exterior. He especially admired the dark gray Galway marble, a limestone packed with white fossils.

As was his custom, he sat toward the back of the empty nave. The organist played the opening chords of a familiar hymn when the choir began to sing. *Rehearsal time*, he thought. Hypnotized by the light streaming through the luminous stained glass over the altar, he watched as it materialized into a shimmering mass. He blinked, and then it assumed a human shape and drifted toward him. Now closer, he recognized Inga's blonde hair and beautiful face, which matched angelic images in the ancient window. She reached out, and blood dripped from her fingertips. Trembling, he recognized the jagged hole above her eyes.

Extending his arm, he felt nothing but air. "Inga, I tried to help," he whispered. "I failed. I'm so sorry. Can you forgive me?" The face began to melt like a wax figure at the end of a horror film. The head, now with sad eyes and a shapeless mouth, nodded.

A loud note from the organ woke him with a jolt. Shaken by the dream, he left and returned to 221B Cook Street. Kara hadn't gotten home yet, so he set her package on the kitchen table and lit the fire under the kettle. He made some tea and went back into the living room. He'd nearly finished his second cup of tea by the time she got home.

"Shit. Look at the time ... nearly four. Sorry, but nothing seemed to go right. I thought the day would never end."

"Don't apologize. You've got a business to run. I'm fine. Just wandered through town and did a little shopping."

"Larsson, you look funny. Did something happen today?"

"Not a lot. Dropped by the cathedral where I enjoyed a free organ recital and nap."

She flashed a playful grin. "I'd nap too, if I ever went, but I do love the Galway marble. When I was six, I snuck a hammer into the cathedral, planning to collect fossils. Michael saw it and threatened my next stop would be the nuns' school if I used it."

"Did you get any fossils?"

"What kind of fool do you take me for, Larsson? Public school was bad enough. Would you like more tea or a Guinness?"

"Guinness would be great."

Kara walked into the kitchen. She returned immediately, holding the brightly colored package. "What's this?"

"Not much, I promise. Open it."

She tore off the colorful paper and opened the box. "Oh, Cal, you shouldn't have, but I'm glad you did. Thank you!"

"Well, I saw you're still using the briefcase from our Longhorn days."

"An old friend and a little frayed, I suppose." She put her arms around his neck and gave him a not-so-sisterly kiss.

Cal enjoyed her thanks, but somehow, it still didn't seem right. It was becoming increasingly apparent that figuring out this new life wasn't going to be easy.

Chapter 15

Call for Help

Cal watched the early morning sky for a hint of light as the car rolled toward Dublin. He hoped this meeting with Kara's friend, the American ambassador, wouldn't be a waste of time. Yesterday, she'd called in a favor, for her study that proved a US Navy vessel had not spilled oil in Dingle Bay.

They arrived at the restaurant and waited. After about fifteen minutes, a tall man with graying hair and forceful blue-gray eyes joined them. Cal knew immediately this was Donovan.

"Patrick, good morning. Wonderful to see you," Kara said, standing to give him a hug.

The man extended his hand to Cal. "You must be the Dr. Larsson Kara told me about. Nice to meet you. I'm Patrick Donavan."

"The pleasure is mine, but Cal is fine."

"Okay, Cal, but please call me Patrick." Donavan's handshake said *Notre Dame fullback*, but his immaculate suit and demeanor said *diplomat*.

"Thank you for meeting us on such short notice."

"Kara said it was important. The little bit she told me about your situation was fascinating."

The waiter arrived with coffee. Looking at Patrick, he asked, "Would you like something, sir?"

"No, thank you. I've had breakfast. Just coffee with a little cream."

Cal began telling the story of how he'd met Inga, gone to the island, and seen her murdered.

"Extraordinary. A person with such a secret could be the object of a considerable interest to a company like ReStemCo, which prides itself on a squeaky-clean image. Do you have proof?"

Cal pulled an envelope from his pocket and handed Patrick the photos from the lab. He looked at them and frowned. "These are worse than I imagined from Kara's description. How could a company like ReStemCo be involved in something so vile? What do you intend to do with them?"

"At the moment, they're my insurance policy. I want to contact ReStemCo and send them copies of the photos as a warning. I want to see the person responsible punished, but at the moment, I'm stumped. Conducting a murder investigation on a Mexican island without hard evidence won't happen."

"And the lab? Do you want to shut it down?"

"Yes. That's what Inga wanted as well. She came to hate what happened to the creatures in the steel wombs."

"But the company is putting out fantastic products. Their stem-cell therapies are helping thousands of people," Kara added.

"So I understand," Patrick said. "A classic dilemma. Their methods are hardly noble, but the fruits of their labor are good. I'm Catholic and know very well the issues usually associated with obtaining embryonic stem cells, and this is even worse. I gather some of the creatures continued to develop and mature?"

"Yes. Some developed past the embryo stage, but they were taken away. Inga didn't know where they went, but the people who took them were German. Inga's friend Bernie Goldman was afraid they might continue to grow into large, fully developed humans … giants. He disappeared before we got back to the island, so I never talked to him. The thing I want most is closure for her family. Patrick, you could help if you'd contact the Swedish ambassador and ask her to request the Swedish Ministry of Foreign Affairs to inform Inga's family of her death. Then have them demand ReStemCo return her body to Sweden. Right now, the family has no idea what's happened."

"I'll make the call when I get to the office."

"That would be wonderful." Cal got up and headed toward the rear of the restaurant. "You'll have to excuse me for a minute. Too much coffee."

After he left, Patrick leaned across the table. "You know more about this than I do. Is he in danger?"

"Honestly, I have no idea. He thinks he may be. Somebody followed Inga and tried to kill her in Italy and finally succeeded on the island. He probably should be concerned."

"He sure as hell should be. People are murdered for less."

When Cal returned, Kara offered him her cup, which had just been filled.

"Thanks, but no more this morning."

Patrick turned and put his hand on Cal's arm. "No question someone wanted Inga dead, but I question whether it was ReStemCo."

"Why?" Cal asked in surprise.

"Certainly, they wouldn't appreciate the publicity your photos would create, but I doubt it would seriously hurt them financially or goad them into murder."

Cal nodded. "That could be, but I can't imagine anyone other than ReStemCo that would have Inga dead. I appreciate your candor, Patrick, and will have to think more about this."

"Good. I'll do everything I can to assist. I have other resources that might be of help. I'll check into them and get back to you."

Patrick got up. As they walked to the door, he shook Cal's hand and gave Kara a kiss on the cheek. "I must be on my way. Nice to meet you, Cal. I'll be in touch soon."

They waved as Patrick's limousine pulled away.

"What now, Larsson? It's too early for a tour of Dublin's bars."

"Let's go the National Museum. As I recall, it's not far, and we can leave the car here."

They arrived at the museum as it opened and spent an hour

wandering through the exhibition halls, which at that moment didn't particularly interest either of them.

"I need some tea. Museums wear me out," she said.

"The last display case we saw gave me an idea. Come this way. We'll see if they'll let us in. Then you'll get tea."

He led her down a hall filled with Celtic artifacts to a small room where an elderly gentleman sat.

"We'd like to examine your Sheela na Gigs."

"You must have already seen them in our exhibit, sir," he said, pointing toward the immense hall behind them. "There are quite a number out there."

"Yes, we saw them, but I'm sure you have more than you can show the public. If possible, I'd like to see them."

"And who might you be, sir?" The guard peered at Cal with a look of renewed interest.

"I'm Dr. Calvin Larsson, a geologist from Sanford College in the States, and this is my associate Kara O'Malley." Cal handed the man his passport.

The guard turned to a computer. "So you are. There's a nice likeness on your college's website. And why are you interested in our Sheela na Gigs, Dr. Larsson?"

"I'm studying the type of rock used to produce them. I hope we will be able to trace early trade routes in western Ireland the same way we use stone tools and arrowheads made by the native tribes of North America."

"And what about your colleague?"

"She's much more familiar with the local geology, which is important in this kind of research."

"Strange I've never heard of this program. Who did you say funds it?"

"The National Science Foundation and a consortium of universities in western Ireland."

"You have until five o'clock. We close then."

"Thank you so much," Cal said as they went into a collections room.

"This cabinet has all our Sheela na Gigs not on display. Just be sure they go back where they belong, and no photos, if you please."

The door closed, and the guard returned to his desk, Kara fell against Cal with unrestrained laughter. "You are so full of bullshit. That was marvelous. I'll never believe anything else you say."

"I was a little worried about the funding part, but all he needs is a story for his computer log."

"Okay, so let's look at these thingamajigs." Kara grinned.

"*Sheela na Gig*. The first one I ever saw was in Bunratty Castle. I've always wanted one for my rock collection, and now that could happen if I pinched one of these.

"Larsson, unless you intend to become a long-term guest of the Republic, I'd suggest you abandon that idea."

"Sorry, just a joke." Cal opened the top drawer of the specimen cabinet and picked out a small female figure carved from limestone. Her legs were spread apart, and her hands rested on her genitals.

"Ugly little thing. What's she doing?"

"She seems to be showing you her private parts."

Kara held it and looked more closely. "Is this a fertility figure?"

"A few experts say so. The more popular explanation is that Sheela na Gigs were used in the thirteenth-century church to warn the faithful about the dangers of sin and lust."

She began to rub against Cal with a slight rotation of her hips. "Works for me."

"I think you're getting the wrong signal from our little Sheela na Gig. They're intended as a warning, not a provocation."

"Are there more?"

"Drawers full. We'll have a look, if you can control your carnal desire."

After they'd looked through most of the drawers, Cal picked up one of the small statues.

"Cal, you're pale. Are you all right?"

He handed it to her.

"Shit, Cal, the dammed thing looks like one of the creatures in your pictures from the lab."

He nodded, bent down, and put the figurine under his heel.

"Don't," Kara warned.

A rotation of his foot turned the Sheela na Gig to powder. "Dust to dust."

"Christ, Larsson, that was crazy." She leaned down, gathering the fragments together into the box that originally held the small figure.

"Just destroyed the ugliest Sheela na Gig in Ireland," he said through clenched teeth.

"I can almost understand, but you could get into serious trouble doing stunts like that. Let's get out of here." She rang the bell, and the guard opened the door.

"Didn't take any souvenirs, did you, lad? You still have three hours."

"That's okay. I've seen enough." Cal dropped his chin and turned away.

"If you want to study the Sheela na Gigs outside of the museum, you'll have to contact the curator, Dr. Ingrid Kelley. Here is her number."

Cal took the slip of paper and kept walking.

As they left the building, Kara spoke. "Larsson, you've got to improve your 'I'm not guilty look' after destroying museum property."

"So true. Let's eat."

"The Black Pig is a block or so away. Their beef and lamb are good, and the salads are outstanding for Ireland."

"Let's do it."

Finishing his third Guinness, he muttered, "I wish getting those creatures from the lab out of my head was as easy as destroying that Sheela na Gig, but I know it was stupid. I should go back and offer to pay for it."

"That would lead the list of the world's most dumb-ass ideas." She laughed.

"Yeah, I guess. Is there a Guinness record for that?"

"Probably." She smiled.

"I made up that stuff about the Sheela na Gigs, but as I went along, it actually sounded like an interesting project. I might come back and talk with Dr. Kelley."

"Stick to photography and painting." She laughed. "You know, it's a long drive back to Galway, and I've just gone past my quota of Guinness. Why don't we stay in Dublin for the night?"

"Are you sure?" he asked.

"I'm sure."

✤

The next morning, Cal woke up early and rolled over. "Kara, how do you perceive God?"

"Larsson, what is your problem?" she stretched, attempting to understand the bewildering question. "How do I perceive God? Is this the beginning of a Sheela na Gigs joke?"

"I'm serious. Is your God the only God?"

"I assume the only way I'm going to shut you up is to play your silly game. Yes, I guess my God is the only true God. Isn't that what the church says?" she asked.

"Can I have the same God?"

"Oh, please."

"Kara, I repeat, can I have the same God as you do?"

She sat up and studied his face. "I'm sure you could, if you still believe in one."

"Can I take communion with you next Sunday?" he asked.

She frowned. "Cal, we've been down this path a few times, haven't we?"

"I guess, but my ideas aren't the same anymore. I was wondering if yours were."

"To tell you the truth, I haven't thought much about it. Not high on my fret list."

"Truth be told, it's not at the top of mine either, but wasn't this one reason we didn't get married years ago?"

She rubbed her eyes. "Okay, I hate to admit it, but yes, it was."

"Weren't your relatives against it because I'm not Catholic?"

"Yes, but most of them are dead now. The rest don't give a damn, and I sure as hell don't."

"So there it is."

"Do you mean one obstacle to our getting married is gone?"

Cal nodded.

"Here we go again. You know it's more than something stupid like religion. Your family in the States, my family and job here. I still don't see it working."

"Kara, did we settle it?"

"What?"

"How we perceive God."

She managed a forced smile. "Larsson, do you see how hilarious this is? Here we are, two people lying in bed together, naked as the day we were born, discussing how we perceive God. We should submit this to the BBC as a new sitcom. The Brits would love it. *Sex and Theology.*"

"A delightful idea, except they'd have to come up with a happy ending."

Chapter 16

All Drowned

During the drive back to Galway, the fog was as heavy as the morning fog filling the valley when he gave Inga the gold Etruscan earrings.

"Larsson, did last night bother you?"

"What do you mean?"

"While we were in bed, did you think of Inga?"

Cal squirmed. "Yes. A little. That's the trouble with emotions. They don't have an off switch. I know you'll have a hard time believing this, but I love you more than ever."

"I'd like to believe that, but …" She tried to think of something more to say, but couldn't. She looked at Cal and realized he was having the same problem.

As soon as they got in the house, Cal heard Kara's fax machine come to life. She went to her office and came back with a sheet of paper. "It's from Judy. You should see this."

"Let's have a look." He started reading and was halfway down the page when he stopped. "Oh, shit!"

"What's the matter?"

"Here." He handed her it to her, pointing to the middle of the page at a September 26 article from the *New York Times*.

Dzilam de Bravo, Mexico—Body of American scientist Bernard Goldman found on beach one mile east of Dzilam de Bravo. He drowned while on a fishing trip.

"That name is familiar. He was Inga's friend, wasn't he?"

"Yes. Never met him, but he was the one worried about embryos evolving into mature individuals that might be able to live outside of the steel wombs. He disappeared before I got to the island."

"You don't believe his death was an accident, do you?"

"Not a chance. He hated fishing, according to Inga."

"So she wasn't the first victim."

"Evidently not. The directors must be desperate to keep what goes on in the lab secret. I need to send ReStemCo an e-mail about my photos and hope they take it seriously."

Kara frowned. "Do you really think that's a good idea right now? So far, they don't know about them, but if they see what you've got, they might really come after you. Remember what Patrick said about someone other than ReStemCo wanting Inga dead. Your photos may not be the insurance policy you think they are."

He looked up. "Hell! I'm not sure, but who else? They stalked her and finally killed her."

"I agree with Patrick. A company that big probably wouldn't be so concerned about negative PR that it would commit murder. An embarrassment, yes, but not a financial catastrophe."

He unfolded Kara's carefully folded fax pages. "If that's true, my little photos aren't worth much. Maybe I should send them to the *New York Times* and try to end ReStemCo's use of the steel wombs to produce stem cells and an army of giants forever. Otherwise, Inga's death will have no meaning."

"If they ever get the idea that's your goal, the risk goes way up."

Cal refolded the fax and tossed it into a trash basket. "Enough about Cal Larsson; this isn't only about me. It's Inga's family that's really important. I can't leave them with this uncertainty. She has to go home. I hope Patrick can help make that happen, but for now, how's your schedule? I need to get away from ReStemCo for a day or so."

"Clear for the next three days. Why?"

"Well, if you have time, maybe we could take a drive out into the countryside around Galway. I've always thought it's one of the prettiest places in Ireland."

"It is, for a fact. Any spot in particular?"

"I'll think about it." He spent the rest of the day trying unsuccessfully to get the island out of his mind.

As the living room clock struck midnight, Kara took Cal's arm. "Time for bed, love."

"Did you check the computer?"

"Three times since we ate!"

Cal tossed for several hours, wrestling the island's demons.

Suddenly, Kara sat up. "Brilliant! I know what I'll do."

He rolled over and yawned. "What did you say?"

"Forget it. Go to sleep. You'll see tomorrow." She laughed and whispered, "And I do mean *see*."

The next morning, he rose early, made coffee, and checked for messages. Nothing had come in, and Kara wasn't up, so he went to a nearby park, where he'd seen a large outcrop of folded limestone. He tried to picture the events that created this structure as a group of children climbed to the top, enjoying geology in their own boisterous way.

When he returned to the house, Kara stood by the window, visibly upset.

"I've been frantic. I thought something happened to you."

"Sorry. I didn't mean to scare you. Just couldn't sleep and needed some fresh air. Anything from cyberspace yet?"

"Good Lord, Larsson! No!"

As quiet filled the room, he sensed she regretted the sharp answer. He took a large glass from the china cabinet and poured in the last of the Jameson's.

"Don't." She grabbed the glass. "I love it too, but this is much too early."

He watched in horror as she emptied the twelve-year-old whiskey into the sink. "God will punish you for that," he said.

"I'm sure she will, but which one? Yours or mine?"

"Probably both." He grinned.

She returned his smile and started breakfast. After they'd eaten, Kara went into her bedroom. Half an hour later, she came out wearing a trench coat. "Go sit on the couch." She stood in front of him. "How would you like to sample Kara's O'Malley's sex therapy?"

"I'll try anything. When?"

"Now!" A throaty laugh followed her coat falling on the floor. She wore nothing but a little red paint in the form of circles around each breast and the outline of a bikini bottom. "Surprise is critical for successful sex therapy. From your expression, I guess that part worked. Stand up!"

"Kara?"

"Quiet! Talking is not allowed." Her hips swayed in serenely erotic undulations. She glided around him, taking his hand and leading him into her bedroom.

An hour later, he lay on his side watching the red-and-pink woman next to him.

"When did you learn to do Kara O'Malley's sex therapy?"

"This morning."

"I love it, but I'm afraid I've ruined your paint job."

She laughed. "Yes, you and my sheets seem to be wearing most of it."

"I hope it's washable."

"Supposed to be."

"Where did you buy it?"

"A shop near the university."

"I'd like to see how the students use the red paint. Go there often?"

"Once, actually. I dropped by after I realized you needed some creative help. I should wash this off before we go out."

"Why? No one will know, unless you plan to go topless."

"If I have an accident, won't the EMS crew enjoy my kinky art?"

"Not as much as I did, I'm sure."

"Good. That's a start. Let me get a shower, and we'll have lunch. Can't play sex therapy all day. Yesterday you said you'd like to take a drive while we wait to hear from Dublin. Have you thought of someplace special you'd like to visit?"

"I've never been to Kilmacduagh, but I saw it in a brochure the other day. Think we could get into the cathedral?"

"I'm sure we can. Been there several times and know where to get a key. We'll leave after lunch," she said, blowing him a kiss on her way to the shower.

They'd only been on the road for ten minutes when Kara glanced at Cal.

"Larsson, is there something wrong with my driving? Was I going too fast?"

"Not at all. Why?"

"You acted like you were looking for the police."

"Nothing like that. Just a case of déjà vu," he said, turning, to look out of the rear window.

"I don't understand. What did you think you saw?"

"A car like the one that followed Inga, but there's nothing now. I'm afraid I'm becoming paranoid." He looked back again and wished it were as simple as that, but he knew he'd seen a black SUV.

The drive from Galway to Gort took half an hour.

Kara went into the Tower B&B. "These folks have the key we'll need to get into the cathedral. All for a two-euro deposit."

Fifteen minutes later, ancient Kilmacduagh Monastery came into view. She left the highway and drove up the lane leading to the seven structures in this seventh-century monastic site.

The black SUV pulled off the road from Gort and climbed the rocky slope. It parked near the top of a small hill, nearly hidden in a small oak grove. The driver grabbed the spotting scope and found a place with a clear view of the ancient ruins. Even from half a mile, she could easily see her quarry.

"Now you'll pay for Inga's death. If you hadn't interfered and taken her from me, she'd still be alive." She adjusted the fine focus. "Vengeance is mine. Isn't that what their Bible says?" she snarled.

Kara stopped in the gravel parking area near the largest building.

"Where to first?"

"Let's start at the round tower. It's the tallest in Ireland," she answered.

Standing at the base of the hundred-foot-tall structure, Cal looked at the door twenty-five feet above him. The aluminum ladder leaning against the wall was just long enough to reach the small opening.

"We're in luck; they must have had a tour yesterday and left it," Kara said.

"Unlucky is more like it. Maybe we should rethink this." He continued staring up at the tiny window that seemed to have gotten higher.

"Come on, Larsson. It's not that bad. And the view from the top is spectacular. I'm doing this for you—even though I'd have thought dancing naked in red paint would be enough for one day," she said, pushing him toward the tower.

Cal started up, but twenty feet off the ground, a breeze shook the ladder.

"Larsson, are you all right?"

"Just peachy." He continued climbing and crawled into the dark room.

"Invigorating, wasn't it?" she said when she got to the window.

"If you say so."

"I don't care for the looks of that, though," she said, pointing to a wooden ladder on the opposite wall.

"Even more exciting than the one outside. Do you suppose it's safe?"

"The lady at the B&B assured me it is. Eight of them between us and the top." She chuckled.

"Whose bright idea was this anyway?" Cal muttered.

"Yours, love."

"We can't go all the way to the top in the dark. Those windows don't let in enough light. We'll break our necks."

"Not so fast, Doctor. You don't get away that easy. I thought ahead. Here," she said, handing him a small flashlight attached to a strap. "Put this on your head like a miner's lamp from our spelunking days in Texas."

Ten minutes later, he climbed off last ladder and joined Kara standing in front of a large window. They gazed down at the shells of six stone buildings and graveyards.

"Fabulous," he said. "Nearly worth the climb. Nearly!"

"According to local folklore, this is where the monks rang handbells, calling people to worship. Probably equally important as fortress and a place to hide the monastery's valuables. Larsson, what's that?"

"A powerful little monocular I started carrying after I got interested in birding. Handy and lighter than binoculars." He fitted it to his eye.

"See anything?"

"Not so far." Then he saw a flash on the low hill beyond the monastic site. "Looks like a reflection off something shiny." He continued scanning the wooded area. "Shit!"

"What's the matter? What's up there?"

"Can't tell for sure, but looks like a black SUV. It's pretty well hidden in the trees. Let's get out of here. Now!" As his foot hit the first rung on the ladder, it splintered, digging into his calf. "Damn hell!"

"Are you all right? What happened?" she asked.

"Damn near broke my neck. I've got to be more careful with these wooden ladders."

"Please do. I can't carry you out of here by myself."

When Cal's feet found the ground, his legs buckled.

"Do you want to sit for a minute? You look a little unsteady." She turned toward the hill and tilted her head. "What's that?"

Cal listened. "Sounds like dogs. Lots of them. Let's move." He grabbed her hand, and they raced through the graveyard, stumbling through an obstacle course of Celtic crosses. "That big stone building with the iron gate is closer than the car. Is that what they call the cathedral?"

"Yes!" she shouted.

As they neared the immense ruin, she tripped, knocking over a wooden angel.

"Quick." He took her arm and kept her from falling with the shattered cherub as they dashed the final twenty feet to the heavy iron gate. "Where's the key?"

"Right here."

He opened the gate, pulled her inside, and slammed it shut. "Let's wait here and see what the barking is all about." As it grew louder, he pointed toward a grassy knoll beyond the tower. Six large dogs emerged over the rise and dashed down the slope. "Damn! They're headed straight toward us."

"Do you think they're dangerous?"

"Hard to know, but let's err on the side of staying alive and not go out." The first dog arrived and lunged, rattling the heavy iron bars and spraying saliva in their direction. Like well-trained soldiers, they took turns attacking the sturdy barrier. Kara covered her eyes in a futile effort to block out the terrifying sight. Led by a huge German shepherd, the dogs circled the ancient building.

"I hope there's not an opening big enough for them to squeeze through."

"Cal, what are we going to do?"

"Did you bring your cell?"

"Of course. Why didn't I think of it?" Kara pulled out the phone and dialed 999. She attempted to explain to the operator what was happening and asked that the police be sent.

The German shepherd continued patrolling the gate, occasionally renewing its attack on the iron bars. Twenty minutes later, two Galway Garda Land Rovers pulled into the parking area. The officers shot into the ground near the crazed animals, trying to scare them. Rather than running away, the dogs charged the police, never pausing after the first one was hit.

Kara turned away. "I can't watch."

Cal wrapped his arms around her, and they stood together until the shooting stopped.

It only took a few minutes before the killing ended, and five corpses lay among blood-splattered tombstones.

One of the Gardaí came to the cathedral gate. "Was anyone hurt?"

Kara wiped her eyes and shook her head. Cal walked over and unlocked the gate.

"Sergeant Kevin O'Byrne," the officer said, shaking Cal's hand.

"I'm Cal Larsson, and this is Kara O'Malley."

The policeman gave her a gentle hug. "Are you all right, lass? I know that was a horrible thing to see."

She attempted a smile. "You'll never know how happy I am to meet you, Sergeant O'Byrne."

"That was one vicious lot. You were lucky to get behind that gate. My priest will love this story. Christians saved from savage beasts by the cathedral. You may make Sunday's sermon."

"Definitely a first," Kara whispered, poking Cal with her elbow.

"In forty years on the force, I've never heard of anything like this. Where did they come from?"

"Up there." Cal pointed to the hill, beyond the tower. "They were pretty far off, but they homed in on us like they'd been programmed. Did you kill them all?"

"No; a big German shepherd escaped. I'm glad you folks weren't hurt."

"What about a pack like that? Is it unusual?"

"Occasionally, we find feral dogs running together, but there was not a feral beast among these. First-class animals, I'd say. Well fed and clean. Quite strange! Almost as if they were being directed, not running wild."

"Sergeant, I have an odd favor to ask. Could a necropsy be done on one the dogs? I'd be willing to cover costs."

"Why? They died of bullet wounds."

"I want to see if something might have been inserted in their brains to make them behave like that."

"Seems a bit farfetched, sir, but since you're paying, I don't see why not. If you're right and the attack was planned, we're dealing with a crime, so we'd better gather all these bodies. After that, I'll take a walk up the hill and try to locate the owner and find the big German shepherd that escaped."

"One more favor. Could you let me know what you discover from the lab work?"

"I'll see to it."

Her greatest achievement was the ability to use tiny computers to control animal behavior. Today, the dogs performed well, but in the end, it went wrong. Barking had taken away the element of surprise, but that could be fixed. Noise wasn't the only problem. She'd started the attack too soon, allowing the man and woman to hide behind the iron door. Timing was critical. She failed, not the dogs. Cursing in German, she sat on a large rock and called a familiar phone number.

"Hello, dear brother. I continue doing your job. First, I eliminated your incompetent lackey, but that was a pleasure. I loathed him for murdering Inga, even though I knew he was obeying your orders. You were so wrong to think her death would return me to you so we could be like we once were." She paused for an answer, which never came. "Oh, you didn't know he was dead? Well, he is." Her mouth formed a twisted smile. "Today, I came close to killing her American lover. He had no business being with her. She was mine. Next time, I will succeed." The snarl startled her, and she dropped the phone. The German shepherd, though fatally injured, was alive and running toward her. The woman reached into her pocket for the control unit, but she was too late. "Apollo, no!"

The large dog leaped for her throat as it had been taught.

Cal and Kara watched as Kevin left the other policemen to finish cleaning up the carnage, and then they started up the hill. He stopped as another sound echoed around them.

Kara jumped. "Did you hear that scream?"

"Yes. It sounded almost human. I'm afraid our nerves are shot. Sorry—poor word choice." Cal's attempt to laugh failed. "We need a drink."

"There's time, if you'd like to stop by O'Sullivans in Kinvara. I've been there once before. It's lovely, and drinks they'll have," Kara said.

"O'Sullivans sounds good." He took her hand, and they walked to the car.

Kinvara was only fifteen minutes away. The pub was a welcome sight, especially after what they'd just witnessed. Cal led her to one of brown leather benches beneath faded posters and newspaper clippings and ordered two pints of Guinness. He asked the waiter if these O'Sullivans were related to Sean and Mary, who lived in nearby Killybegs. No one seemed to know. They went outside and found a bench facing Kinvara Bay as they watched the sky fade to a canvas of pastel pinks.

Cal was considering his empty glass when a strong hand clamped down on his shoulder. He turned, coming face-to-face with Sean O'Sullivan, who pulled him up from the bench and gave him a rib-cracking hug. "It's good to see you, Sean, and I'm happy your arm healed," he snorted, giving his ribs a theatrical touch.

Kathleen stood next to her father. "Don't I get a hug?"

"My dear little Gaelic mountain goat, yes, of course you do." Cal lifted her and kissed her forehead.

An elbow reminded him that Kara stood beside him. "Forgive me. Meet my friend Kara O'Malley." This set off another round of hugs. "I knew someone this pretty must be Irish," Sean said. "Didn't I say so, Mary?"

Mary, who was standing behind Kathleen, nodded.

"Sean, how did you happen to be here?" Cal asked.

"I didn't happen to be here. I came after I got a call from the bartender, saying a Brit was looking for me. During the bad times, a message like that was reason enough to check. Old IRA families never completely lose their suspicious nature, but from what Jimmy said, I thought it might be you, not a bloody Brit. So here we are."

"I'm delighted, but Jimmy must not be very good at recognizing accents."

"Poor bugger's half-deaf."

Kara sat next to Kathleen, who talked nonstop about how Cal had saved her in Iceland. Her mother added her thanks.

Kara snickered and gave him another elbow. "Larsson, you seem to be quite the hero."

"Oh, he is," Kathleen added with delight.

Cal motioned for the bartender to bring more drinks and started telling the O'Sullivans about their day. Kara, who didn't want to relive the morning, excused herself and took Kathleen with her. Sean seemed more than casually interested in the attack at the Kilmacduagh Monastery.

"I work in the prosecutor's office in Killybegs, and I know Kevin O'Byrne. I hope they get that German shepherd and discover who owned those dogs. I'll make sure they do the necropsy you want."

"Thanks, Sean. I appreciate you coming over to see us. Next time, we'll make sure our visit is longer," Cal said as Kathleen and Kara returned.

"It had better be." Kathleen smiled and then blurted, "When are you and Kara getting married?"

"Kathleen O'Sullivan, you have no manners." Mary gave her a playful smack on the head. "That's none of your business."

"You'll get an invitation as soon as I find out," Cal said.

Kara grimaced as Sean and Mary exchanged awkward looks and began a final round of hugs and good-byes.

"Time to go home and see if the computer has news for you," Kara said.

"I'd almost forgotten."

"That's a good sign."

As soon as she got into the house, Kara went to her office. "Come see what Patrick sent."

Cal opened Patrick's e-mail and read aloud, "Have important information. See attachments."

The first five weren't particularly interesting. After reading the last one, he slumped and shook his head.

"Cal, what is it? You look like you've seen a ghost." She moved closer and read the message from the October 7 *Dallas Morning News* that seemed to stun him.

> Yucatán Peninsula, Mexico—Dzilam de Bravo, Mexico: Theoclymernus Papakonstandinou drowns in boating accident near the town of Dzilam de Bravo. Ten miles from Mérida: Jack Archer, formerly with the Dallas police, was found dead, apparently killed by a pack of wild dogs.

"You can be sure these weren't accidents," Cal said. "Damn it! Theo got me off that cursed island and tried to save Inga. Never should have left without him."

"Why would they kill Archer?" She stood behind him and rubbed his shoulders. "Wasn't he one of them?"

"Maybe he became a liability. From what I saw, he was nuts."

"You haven't opened everything." He scrolled down the list of e-mails and found one from Mark Svendson.

> Just got a call from Frederick Rundstrom. He said ReStemCo is flying Inga's body to Sweden tomorrow. The funeral will be later in the day.

Kara asked, "What are you going to say to her family? She was shot attempting to escape from her employer."

"I've thought a lot about that. Since ReStemCo didn't give much of an explanation, I suppose the story will be that she died during an unfortunate laboratory accident. It happened after I left the island, so I don't know all the details."

"You're pale. I'm sorry, Cal. I wasn't thinking when I asked."

"That's okay. I'm fine. I'll fly to Sweden early tomorrow."

"Would you like me to join you?"

"Yes, very much. That will be the worst part of the whole affair, won't it?"

"It will be."

It was ten o'clock that night when Cal sat down in front of Kara's computer. "I need to learn more about ReStemCo. I'll be finished by the time you get a shower."

It wasn't long until the answers danced across the monitor. ReStemCo had been purchased five years earlier by Forschung Deutsch Zelle AG (ZFD), a German company whose research included human cell growth. ZFD's first board, in the 1930s, had been made up of Joseph Mengele, Aribert Heim, Eduard Wirths, and Horst Schumann, all of whom went on to become infamous as Nazi war criminals. Many of their grandchildren were on the current board. *A notorious group of thugs*, Cal mused. He'd nearly finished when he noticed another name. "What the hell!"

Aryanne Wolf had been a ReStemCo executive and an expert on miniaturized computers. She'd gained fame for successfully creating robotically manipulated cockroaches used to locate victims in collapsed buildings. Cal shook his head. This must have been after Inga last saw her. Aryanne's brother, Adolph later joined the firm and headed the security division.

Kara returned from her shower and leaned over Cal, who studied the monitor. "This fills in a few more pieces to the puzzle," he said.

She shook her head and looked at Cal, confused by what she'd read. Before she could say anything, the phone rang. After a moment, she handed the receiver to Cal. "For you. Sean O'Sullivan says it's something you should know about the dog attack today."

He took the phone and switched on the speaker mode.

"Hello, Cal. I know it's late, but I thought you'd be interested."

"What have you found?"

"I just got a call from Kevin O'Byrne. After you had gone, he decided to find out where the dogs came from. The German shepherd that escaped was wounded and left a trail of blood. O'Byrne found it dead."

"Good. It won't hurt anyone now. I guess that ends the story."

"Not quite. It was lying next to a black Mercedes SUV. Here's the unbelievable part. A woman was between the dog and SUV. Her throat had been torn open by the dog before it died."

"What did she look like?"

"Sturdy build, short white hair. Her German driver's license identified her as Aryanne M. Wolf from a place called Backer Villen. A cell phone and a device resembling an elaborate TV remote were near the body. She must have been watching you."

"Why so?"

"A powerful spotting scope was sitting on a rock with a clear view of the Kilmacduagh site. One more thing: there were six large cages in the SUV. They almost certainly carried the dogs that came after you."

"Thanks, Sean. I'll get back to you later."

Cal stared at the phone, trying to make sense of what he'd heard. Kara brought two glasses of Jameson's.

"Thought you could use this."

"Yes. More than you know."

Kara sat down. "Have you heard of this Aryanne person?"

"Yes. Inga told me about a German cousin, Aryanne Wolf, who wanted to be her lover. She seemed to genuinely care for Inga and may have murdered the man who raped Inga when she was fourteen. For some reason, she followed us through Tuscany and Sweden, but Inga never saw her, just the car—a black SUV. And get this: she worked for the German company that bought ReStemCo."

"Inga never told you that?"

"No. I doubt she knew about it, but it may explain why she was hired by ReStemCo. She was caught in a web built by a spider named Aryanne."

"Why did she stalk you and Inga?"

Cal shook his head. "Maybe she was worried about Inga. Trying to keep her safe."

"Safe from what?"

Cal raised his eyebrows and shrugged. "I wish I knew."

"Okay. Then why did she try to kill us today?"

"It may have been payback for me being something she could never be—Inga's lover. A lot of the puzzle is still missing, but I'll not solve it tonight. I'm exhausted. Let's turn in."

He took Kara's hand, and they went into the bedroom.

Chapter 17

Home to Sweden

Cal's mood was cheerless during the trip to the funeral in Kristianstad. He knew he was lousy company, but he realized Kara understood. His conflicted thoughts felt like a dead weight as the church's gravel parking lot crunched under the Saab's tires. He saw Mark standing with a group of people who he recognized from Inga's photographs as her sisters and brother. Mark walked slowly to car; both were silent as they embraced. Mark went to the other side of the car.

Kara got out and touched his arm. "Hi. I remember you. We met once in Austin."

"Hi, Kara. I'm glad you came. Cal will need you today."

"I know, but I'll wait here for now."

The two men approached Inga's family.

"This is Cal Larsson, the American I told you about. Cal, this is Kerstin Marie, Ann Marie, and Marie Louise."

Cal gave each a hug. Ann Marie took his hand, but it was several minutes before she could talk, as tears blocked her voice. "We understand you helped have Inga returned to us. Please know, we thank you."

He smiled but could only nod his answer.

A man with Inga's handsome features and blond hair stepped forward. Cal needed no introduction. This was her brother, Frederick, who reluctantly extended his hand but didn't seem pleased to greet this American.

"There is someone else," Frederick said.

They walked to a car with black crepe draped across the hood. Cal realized the old woman inside was Inga's mama. Even in her eighties, she radiated the family's good looks. She got out of the car and embraced Cal.

"Mrs. Rundstrom, I'm so sorry. Inga was a wonderful person. We were good friends, and I miss her." He struggled with emotion as Mark translated.

Taking his hand, the old woman answered quietly in Swedish.

"She's glad Inga had a friend there when she died. Inga was a good daughter and happy doing work she loved—work that helped people," Mark said.

Cal gave her a hug, and everyone walked to the church.

After the service, the coffin was carried to the family plot. Cal and Kara looked down into the newly dug hole.

"Kara, give me a minute."

She squeezed his hand and returned to the parking lot.

With eyes closed, he remained standing by the open grave. "Inga, I'll never forget how we were together. I'll do everything I can to close the lab. That's what you wanted, wasn't it?"

Turning to leave, he noticed Frederick watching from a distance. Cal sensed some of his anger now lay in the ground with his sister.

"Dr. Larsson, may I have a word?"

"Sure."

They turned away from the grave and moved farther from the other mourners.

"When Inga came home, I was the one asked to identify her. The coroner believed her head wound looked odd and commented someone had done considerable cosmetic work on it. He asked if I knew anything other than there had been a laboratory accident. All I could answer was something horrible happened that day. Is there more?"

Cal shoulders slumped as he nudged a piece of sod with the toe of his shoe. "There is."

They paused by the grave, while Cal quietly explained events on the island that awful night.

Frederick knelt and threw a handful of dirt on the wooden box. "What will happen to the one who murdered Inga?"

"He's been killed. I'm afraid that's as much justice as she'll get."

"My sisters and Mama do not need to know any of this, do they?"

"I don't see why."

The two men shook hands, and Cal rejoined Kara. His explanation to Frederick was only partially true. There was more to her murder, much of it he still didn't understand. At least he'd succeeded in returning Inga home.

Chapter 18

Great Blasket

Back in Kara's living room, Cal searched for something to read, but dragging his mind away from the Kristianstad cemetery was hopeless. Kara brought him a cup of coffee.

"I guess you want to be alone," she said.

Before she could leave, he took her hand. "Going with me yesterday means more than I can tell you. It reminded me how good we are together."

"Larsson, I—"

"Kara, I've loved you since the day we met."

Her mouth worked into a wry smile. "I'm nearly fifty and pretty well set in my ways—my company, our families, religion. I just don't think—"

But he didn't let her finish. "So? I'm fifty-five and I'm sure more set in my ways than you are. On my trip to Iceland, I thought how much I'd like to have someone there sharing it with me. To see and do things together. Haven't you ever wanted that?"

Kara moved closer, touching his hands. "My life here is good. I'm near family. The people and place I love most on Earth. I could never move to America. And you! You love those nieces of yours like daughters. It would be impossible for you to live anywhere but there."

"I understand all that, but today flying is cheap enough. We'd be like the snowbirds in the States."

"Snowbirds?"

"Americans who spend summers up north, winters in the south. They fly back and forth, like migrating birds. Summers in Ireland, winters in North Carolina. Why not?"

"Larsson! You insist on making this difficult, don't you?"

"Doing my best. When I met Inga, I said to myself, 'Cal, the Irish girl will never say yes, and you're not getting any younger.' Could be, now's the time to move on. If Inga hadn't been killed, we might have gotten married, but I couldn't shake the nagging fear your memory would always be there. I don't know whether it would have worked for Inga and me. I'll never know, but I don't want to live forever in a world of what might have been."

She looked down and whispered in a voice filled with feeling, "I understand what you're saying, but I need more time to think."

"Fine, but please don't take another twenty years." He thought for a minute. "There are two days before I leave for home. Let's go someplace where there are no round towers or killer dogs."

She studied his face and nodded with a jolt of her chin. "Okay. How about the Great Blasket?"

"What's a Great Blasket?"

"A place you visited ten years ago but apparently don't remember."

"I'm afraid you're right."

"Come on, Larsson. You loved it. Said you wanted to go back and take the boat to the island."

"Is it that the one at the end of the Dingle Peninsula? It's fuzzy. Didn't we just go to the Great Blasket Centre with the amazing little museum?"

"Right, but this time let's really experience the Great Blasket. It would do you good. I was on the advisory council for a lot of years and can find my way around like a native. We could spend the night in Killarney or Dingle and indulge ourselves with seafood. The best in this part of Ireland."

"Okay, let's do it."

They packed two overnight bags and tossed them in the trunk. Kara drove, allowing him to enjoy the scenery. An hour later, they parked at the Cliffs of Moher, with its vertical drop of six hundred feet.

"This beats the California coast, plus no tourists," he said, walking to the edge for a better view and attaching another lens to his new camera.

She followed him around for fifteen minutes before turning back. "I see you still take more pictures than anyone I've ever known."

"It's what I do."

"I'll see you in the car." She returned to the car and started the engine.

"Give me a minute."

"One minute it is, but it's near lunchtime, and the clock's running." She laughed.

In Killarney. they went to a pub she knew well from visiting the Great Blasket. The fish and chips were the best he'd had since arriving in Europe.

"I'm glad you remembered where this place was," Cal said.

"I've been here too often to forget."

Soon they arrived in Dingle with its brightly painted houses and the distinction of being the most westerly town in Europe.

"We could stay here, if we're late getting off the island," she said.

Ten minutes later, they arrived in Dunquin and drove into the empty parking lot reserved for ferry passengers going to the Great Blasket.

"I hate to see this," she said.

"What's wrong?"

"No cars. If the project is to succeed, we need visitors coming here. Could be the rotten economy."

"What project?"

"I'll explain later, but let's go. Look at the sky," she said, pointing to the dark clouds gathering over the island. "We'd better hurry."

They walked to the small dock and were met by a man whose weathered features confirmed his many years on the water.

"Good morning to you, Miss O'Malley. Haven't seen you recently."

"Happy to be back. Captain Brody MacAleese, this is my friend Cal Larsson, another geologist. He's visiting from the States. I want to show him our island."

"Miss O'Malley here used to give tours around the island, explaining how the rock formed. Where in the States is home?"

"North Carolina."

"My uncle Sean lives there, near the mountains."

"A smart man, your uncle. Much cooler there in the summer than my part of North Carolina."

"Captain, are we the only ones here?" Kara asked.

"Sadly, yes. No one else all day."

"Sorry to hear that," she said.

"It's fine. Probably the forecast for filthy weather kept people home. Come up here and join me in the cockpit. You'll be more comfortable." They sat in relative comfort, happy to be out of the cold wind for the two-mile ride across open water, now stirred into angry whitecaps.

"Thanks. It's much better in here. The council should get a cover for your boat so all the passengers can stay warm and dry on days like this."

"That they should, lass. Please tell the bloody skinflints. But if you would, leave my description of them out of it."

"I still know most of the members and have called them worse."

"From the looks of it, the trip back may be bumpy." MacAleese peered toward the billowing clouds over the Great Blasket. "You should get back to the boat as fast as you can. Here, you might need these." He handed them two lightweight slickers.

"Maybe we shouldn't go, with a storm coming in," Cal said.

"You'll be fine, but get back to the boat before dark. That's when things may get exciting."

MacAleese secured the mooring lines, and they jumped onto the dock.

"See you soon, Captain. Kara called over her shoulder.

They climbed up the rocky path from the beach to the village.

"A ghost town. Where are the people?" Cal asked.

"A livelihood here became impossible. One by one, they left. The last ones moved out in 1953, after three hundred years of continuous habitation."

"If the villagers are gone, who will live here?"

"No one. We hope to create a living museum." She leaned against one of the derelict buildings, loosening a stone that landed on her foot. "Damn!" She glared at the offending rock before returning it to the crumbling wall. "Gives you an idea how much work needs to be done, but that takes money. Two years ago, we applied for a grant from the Office of Public Works for restoration to continue."

"So this is the Great Blasket project. You should bring them up here barefoot."

She gave him a half grin. "Do you remember why this place is so important to Ireland?"

"Didn't the people here speak both Gaelic and English and write in Gaelic about life on the island?"

"Something even more important than that."

Cal squinted and looked toward the darkening sky for an answer. "Aren't they among the best examples of traditional Irish storytelling written in Gaelic?"

"Can you tell me any of their names—those people who wrote those books?"

"Even if I could remember, I couldn't pronounce them."

"Listen and learn, Larsson—Tomás Ó Criomhthain, Muiris Ó Súilleabháin, Seän O Duinnshleibhe. Music to your ears."

"It is musical. You're pretty good, but aside from pronouncing unpronounceable names, can you really speak Gaelic?"

"A little, but not like my brother, Mike, and sister, Eileen."

"I do appreciate how important Gaelic is to your cultural identity."

"That it is. More than most Americans could understand. We'd better crack on. With that sky, we shouldn't overextend our stay."

After a ten-minute walk, they made it to the top of the nine-hundred-foot mountain that loomed over the Great Blasket.

"Breathtaking, isn't it?" she asked.

Cal took in the panorama of green slopes, jagged cliffs, and white beaches.

"Over there!" She pointed across the water as a double rainbow pierced the bank of clouds spreading across the Dingle Peninsula.

"Ireland deserves two names: the Emerald Isle and the Rainbow Isle," he said.

She nodded and continued up the hill. "One more stop. The Dún Beag Fort is something you shouldn't miss."

"You're right; if it's a fort, I don't want to miss it."

"This one isn't as large as Dún Aonghasa on the Aran Islands, but the walls are over a thousand years old. Let's hurry." She pulled on his arm as lightning lit the horizon.

They passed four defensive banks and walked through the opening in the massive dry stone rampart.

Cal rubbed his hand over the moss-covered rock as his head jerked up. "Didn't the captain say no one else is on the island today?"

"That's true. Why?"

He nodded toward the wall on their right. "Something or someone moved."

"Could be a caretaker from the mainland. They come over in their own boats to work on the buildings. They use an inlet on the other side of the island, but I can't imagine them being here on a day like this. Shall we press on?" She grabbed his arm again.

He looked back at the wall in an attempt to forget what he thought he'd seen. *I know damned well it was more than movement; it was two people*, he thought. "Come on, Kara. Let's head for the boat."

"It's just a little bit farther. You really must see it."

Cal caught up and stood next to her where the land ended in a sheer drop to the Atlantic. "This is impressive. Nobody's getting in from this direction. Where does this path go?"

"Down, and then along the cliff to the other side of the fort. Halfway, there are runic inscriptions, but I'm warning you—it's narrow and a hell of a drop if you leave the path."

"I really think it's time to leave, but what the hell—runic inscriptions? In for a penny, in for a pound."

After a few minutes, they were below the fort's stone walls. The trail had been widened in modern times and a metal railing added, but there was no protection from the wind or salt spray it carried.

"The wind is picking up. Stay close to the cliff," he said.

"Any closer and I'll be part of it." She held on to his arm but abruptly swung around, touching a finger to her lips. Her eyes motioned upward.

"What?" he whispered. At first all he could hear was the howling wind. With no warning, dirt and rock cascaded across the path. He leaned back against the railing and looked up; trying to see what caused it.

"Shit, Larsson, don't do that. You'll kill yourself."

Cal's eyes stung from the ocean spray, but he could still make out a man standing above them. Cal blinked and was shocked to see the mysterious little man with flaming red hair and pointed goatee from his first night in Chez ReStem.

The man called down. "Hello, Dr. Larsson."

Cal strained to hear over the wind and yelled, "I remember you from the island!"

"I remember you, as well. You killed my sister."

"What are you talking about? I don't know your sister and sure as hell didn't kill her."

"Who is this guy?" Kara begged, pleading for explanation.

"I have no idea, except that he's a nutcase." Cal repeated his question as loudly as he could.

The answer drifted down, obscured by the howling wind. "She was the woman with white hair."

Cal and Kara looked at each other as the wind struggled to blow them off the path into the Atlantic. "I'll come up and talk," Cal called.

"I'm so sorry, Dr. Larsson, but you're not coming up here. You are nothing but an annoying insect." A second shape stepped from the shadows—a giant carrying a huge stock block. "And you should know my large friend here hates insects."

"Jesus, Larsson, what the shit is going on?" Kara stepped back against the cliff wall.

Cal watched the giant lift the rock above his head. He stood poised to drop it on them when the ledge under his feet broke with a loud crack echoing a distant clap of thunder and illuminated with a flash of lightning. Both the giant and the redheaded man catapulted off the cliff, falling past Cal and Kara. The man's face contorted as he reached out to grab the metal railing, his arms and legs flailing until he disappeared into darkness. Cal barely saw the giant's face, but it looked like a horror mask with partially formed features.

"If the devil exits, we've just seen him," Cal said.

Kara stood frozen, too frightened to respond.

"I'm sure that was one of the giants from Inga's lab. That lab must be shut down, one way or another. Come on." He clutched her arm while they staggered up the trail to the top of the cliff, through the passage in the thick stone wall, and out of the fort. They stumbled down the hill toward the waiting boat.

Captain MacAleese met them the dock.

"You two seem in a bit of a rush," he joked.

"Please, Captain, let's get to Dunquin as fast as possible," Cal said.

MacAleese started the engine and cast off. "Sit and tell me what happened up there."

Kara sat in stony silence, holding her hands to her face, while Cal did his best to explain what had happened in the fort.

"I watched you going up the hill," the captain said, "and thought I saw other people, but I couldn't be sure in this light. Eventually decided it was just bushes dancing in the wind. I'll phone the police. They'll want to search for the bodies. Hang on. It's going to be bumpy."

The wind tossed cold spray over the boat. Cal held Kara tight, attempting to warm her shivering body.

"Miss O'Malley, the chief constable would like to speak with you," MacAleese said, handing her the phone.

"Do you want me to talk to him?" Cal asked.

She blinked and handed Cal the phone.

After finishing the call, he put his arm around her again. "The chief constable wants to talk to us as soon as we get back. Needs to know exactly what happened out there, but in this weather, they won't be searching for bodies until morning."

When the boat docked, Captain MacAleese hugged Kara. "I'm sorry you had such a visit. Go to town, and have yourselves a drink. Please come back soon and tell me more about the island's rocks."

She kissed him on the cheek. "I will when it's warm and sunny. Then we can work on wringing euros out of Dublin for the village and your boat," she said with a warm smile.

They drove to the police station. As they walked to the door, Cal turned and looked at Kara. "Are you okay doing this now?"

"I think so. Let's get it over with."

A short man limped forward, his back curved but his eyes vivid and bright. "You must be the famous Miss O'Malley and Dr. Larsson," he said, his voice deep. "I'm Ryan Brennan."

"We are. This is Kara, and I'm Cal, but why famous?" Cal asked.

"*In*famous might be more the truth. Two days ago, I read Sergeant O'Byrne's report about the incident at Kilmacduagh with the dogs. Seems like you two are getting quite a reputation in the west of Ireland. Come into my office and tell me everything. I make the best tea in Dunquin."

An hour later, he walked with them to the street. "Tomorrow we'll have boats in the water and teams searching the island. Those two who fell off the cliff must have used a boat to get over. We need to find it and them, if possible. I know how to reach you if I have more questions."

They shook hands, and Cal and Kara returned to Kara's car.

"Cal, would you mind driving?"

"Glad to. Let's find a room in Dingle and then eat."

After a few minutes, the Dingle Inn's sign flickered in the distance. Cal went in to register for the night. He came back and stuck his head in the car window.

"We're all set, except that the room only has twin beds."

After a quick dinner, they shared one of the twin beds and tried to put the Great Blasket out of their minds.

The next morning, back in the restaurant, Cal and Kara took the same table they had shared the night before when they'd feasted on lobster and oysters.

"Today is beautiful," the waitress said. "Just for you. Nicer than yesterday, to be sure. You'd better be hungry; our omelets and rashers are smashing. Would you like a little more of our best Irish whiskey? You seemed to like it well enough last night."

Kara shook her head. "I make it a rule to never ever hit the good stuff before noon."

The waitress grinned and returned to the kitchen.

On the way back to Galway, they drove past the Cliffs of Moher. "Cal, do you want any more pictures?"

"Nope. Let's go home."

As they approached Galway, Kara turned. "I never thanked you for saving my life in Kilmacduagh and now on the island."

"Thank me?" He laughed. "If not for me, you'd never have been in danger in the first place." He paused, uncertain how to continue. "I love you, you know, and only hope it's not too late for us."

"Larsson, you're more important to me than you think, but have you forgotten Inga? I doubt if you will ever be able to."

This wasn't how he'd hoped for the conversation to begin. He spent the remainder of the drive trying to enjoy the Irish countryside and forget the Great Blasket.

Early the next morning, Kara received an urgent call from a client reporting a pollution problem near the River Corrib.

"Another leaky fuel storage tank on one of the bloody farms." She slipped into her boots. "It's your last day here, and I wanted to spend it with you."

"Will you be gone all day?"

"I don't think so." She kissed him and left.

He showered, put on the robe Kara had bought for him, and made another cup of coffee. He sat at her computer to check his e-mails and pass the time till she returned. Then he decided to do a search for Aryanne Wolf. Inga knew she had a brother, and now here was a photograph of Adolph Wolf standing next to a white-haired lady with her back to the camera. Cal moved closer to the computer monitor.

"That's the redheaded freak who tried to kill us on the Great Blasket and the same person I saw in Chez ReStem on the island in an animated conversation with Archer," he muttered to the computer. Cal felt a knot in his stomach. He had nearly forgotten about the note Theo found ordering Archer "to take care of her." Theo was sure it was an order to kill Inga, signed by someone named Adolph. That night on the beach, Archer succeeded.

Cal already knew that before joining Forschung Deutsch Zelle AG, Aryanne trained guard dogs and worked with miniaturized computers. *With that background, she sure as hell might have been able to create robotically manipulated dogs like the pack that came after Kara and me in Kilmacduagh.* He shut the computer down and made a phone call to Dublin.

By ten o'clock, the blue sky was replaced by black clouds. He walked to the window and watched a white oak in the backyard bend under the wind gusts, accompanied by torrential rain. *I hope she's not been out in this,* he thought when he heard a noise in the living room. "Kara, is that you?"

"It's me." She stomped into the kitchen, leaving a trail of muddy water in her wake.

Cal's attempt to stifle a smile failed. "I'm sorry. Did you get caught in the storm?"

"Did I get caught in the fucking storm? Hell no, Larsson! I took a drive in the river and forgot to close the windows. Of course I got caught in the damned rain! I was so busy taking soil samples. I never paid any mind to the weather till the lightning and wind. Then it came bucketing down."

"Here, let me hold you." He took off the bathrobe he'd been wearing and wrapped it around her. She shivered as water trickled off her auburn bangs. "I'm freezing. I've got to get out of these clothes."

"Can I help?"

"Be quick about it." Kara's clothes soon formed soggy piles around their feet while they snuggled in the robe.

"Glad I got this in large," she said.

"Here we stand, two peas in a pod." He laughed.

"Two bods in a robe," she corrected.

"Kara, you must know we're perfect for each other," he said, touching her body.

She twisted away. "Please! We had a remarkable week, one I'll never forget, but maybe we should leave it at that. You can drop by again after your next adventure."

"Can't we talk about it?"

"Not now. You'll be gone tomorrow."

"I love you and want to be with you, whether here or in the States. I don't care anymore. Marry me, or we can just live together if you'd rather. Hell, I might even become Catholic." He waited for a response as her eyes glistened with emotion.

She slipped out of the robe and left for the shower. Cal stared at the closed door.

An hour later, she returned with a fresh pot of coffee.

"Have a seat while I tell you what I learned today," Cal said, patting the couch. He attempted to explain as dispassionately as he could.

Kara set her cup on the table and took his hand. "That's absolutely unbelievable and awful. What a pit of vipers Inga landed in. So who actually murdered her?"

"Archer may have pulled the trigger, but it was because Aryanne's brother wanted Inga dead."

"I'm confused. Why did he want to kill Inga? That still makes no sense. What could have been his motive?"

"We'll never know, since Aryanne and Adolph are both dead."

"This is all so outrageous. Isn't it too much of a coincidence for Inga and Aryanne to have worked for the same company?"

"Maybe it wasn't a coincidence at all. Aryanne was obsessed with Inga and wanted to be her lover. I asked Inga how she got the job with ReStemCo. One day, a letter arrived in her office at the university, asking if she'd be interested in groundbreaking research at a world-class laboratory in a warm climate. It sounded too good to turn down. I'm sure Inga had no idea Aryanne was behind her getting the job."

"Did Aryanne work on the island?"

"I never saw her there."

"So how would getting Inga a job there help Aryanne become her lover?"

"She was high up in the company that owned ReStemCo and could have moved to the island anytime she wanted. With Inga locked into a job there, maybe Aryanne thought she would at last have a chance to encourage a relationship. There's something else. She and her brother both worked for Forschung Deutsch. He was also involved in hush-hush research on humans. I have no proof, but I'd guess the two of them may have used the mistakes from the island to produce robotically manipulated humans."

"The giant on the cliff, in Dún Beag Fort?"

"Yes," Cal said.

"What a nightmare!" Kara said. "One thing I still don't understand. Why did Adolph Wolf try to kill us on the Great Blasket?"

"He may have seen me as a threat to his perverse scheme."

"They were both totally insane. How about Irish whiskey?"

"Perfect."

She returned with two glasses, one with ice. After their glasses were emptied, she took his hand and pulled. "It's late, and you should get some sleep. You have an early flight tomorrow."

Chapter 19

Good-Bye, My Love

Cal opened the window and took a deep breath of the air washed clean by yesterday's storm. He packed his bag, which wasn't much larger than the one he'd bought in Mérida the day he left Mexico.

Kara stood in the doorway. "You need some breakfast to travel on. Would you like eggs, bacon, and tomatoes?"

"Sounds wonderful," he replied even though he knew he wouldn't taste a thing.

Somewhere in the house, the telephone rang, and she disappeared to answer it. In a moment, she was back.

"It's Patrick. Says to put the speaker on. Okay?"

"Sure." He stepped close to her as she held the receiver. "Hello, Patrick. Thanks for returning my call. How are you?"

"Fine, Cal. I wanted to wish you bon voyage, and there's something else. Yesterday, I had lunch with an old friend from my Langley days and mentioned ReStemCo. His interest surprised me."

Cal whispered into Kara's ear, "Langley, Virginia—home of the CIA." Her eyes narrowed.

"Did he say why?" Cal asked.

"Not so much about ReStemCo as the German company that now owns it."

"Yes, I know. Forschung Deutsch Zelle AG."

"Seems the intelligence community at large is interested in them. Britain's MI5, Ireland's G2, Germany's BfV—all of them. Something to do with terrorism, but either he wasn't sure how or had to keep his mouth shut."

"Did Adolph Wolf's name come up?"

"Indeed. They seem keen to learn as much as they can about him."

"Did you know that Wolf's uncle Markus once headed the East German Stasi?"

"My friend knew that too. Adolph Wolf was apparently a genius, with degrees in medicine and computer science, but also quite mad. In addition to his research, he ran security for Forschung Deutsch Zelle AG. Seems something beyond manufacturing embryonic stems cells was going on at the island. Do you know anything about that?"

"Yes," Cal said. "Some of the embryos began to grow into fully formed human giants. These creatures didn't stay long in the lab or the island. They were shipped out to someplace called Backer Villen. Did your friend mention that?"

"No, but I'm sure he'll be interested. My God, Cal, what else do you know?"

"A little. Tell your friend that Wolf had a sister, Aryanne."

"They know as well, and there are rumors he enjoyed being intimate with her."

"You mean, having sex?"

"Yes, and there's more to Aryanne," Patrick answered.

"There sure is, but since your friend is so well informed, I suppose he's aware Aryanne was an expert on miniaturized computers, which she used to control robotically manipulated cockroaches. It was written up in *Science News* a while back. Two days ago, Kara and I were attacked by a pack of her dogs at Kilmacduagh. One went rogue and killed Aryanne. I think she used miniaturized computers to turn them into killer canine drones. I asked Kevin O'Byrne, a sergeant with the Gardaí, if they would have a necropsy done on one of the dogs and send me the results. Your G2 friend may want to pursue this."

"He will find it very interesting. This sounds more and more like a Gothic horror tale."

"Worse! One last thing, and it's important. We went to the Great Blasket two days ago. Nearly got killed by a red-haired man who I'm sure was Adolph Wolf. Another man—a huge man—was helping him. They both ended up in the Atlantic at the bottom of the cliff. G2 might check to see if the Dunquin police found any bodies."

"Most unbelievable story I've ever heard. I'm sure they will be appreciative. Please tell me there isn't anything else."

Cal laughed. "Not yet."

"By the way, you may get a call from Langley, with a job offer after you return to North Carolina. Give me a ring the next time you visit Ireland. You're much more interesting than the average American tourist."

"Way too interesting for me. Good-bye, Patrick, and thanks for everything."

"Good-bye. You two be safe."

"You never mentioned to Patrick that Inga and the Wolfs were cousins," Kara said.

"No point. It would only cause her family hours of painful questioning, and I'm sure they wouldn't be of any help to the spooks."

"Why would this interest all those security agencies anyway?"

"Killer dogs as drones, unquestioning giants with great strength and no history—I'm sure terrorists could find something to keep them busy. After our intelligence community digests this, the island's steel wombs will be out of business."

"So Inga's death and your photos weren't meaningless after all."

"So it would seem," Cal said through clenched teeth. "The irony is Inga's death really had nothing to do with the island's giant embryos factory, financial loss to stockholders, or corporate embarrassment. It had everything to do with the incestuous love of a deranged madman for his sister. Adolph was jealous of Inga, his rival for Aryanne. Now it's a closed book, and that's fine with me."

She put her arms around him. "It's time. We should go."

A restrained quiet joined them on the ride to Shannon Airport. The Aer Lingus jumbo jet circling overhead reminded Cal he'd soon be home in North Carolina and Kara would be here in Ireland.

Too bad I lost Iceland's magic pebbles, he thought. *I could use them now.*

She parked and walked into the terminal with him. They found a coffee bar and ordered two cappuccinos.

"What's on your iPad?" she asked.

"A book by Asa Larsson. Should be enough to get me home."

"Swedish mystery writer, isn't she? Another cousin?"

"Not that I'm aware of, but I guess there are loads of unknown Larsson cousins."

"I need the ladies'. I'll be back before your flight is called." Kara forced a smile.

"I hope so." He stirred another sugar into his cappuccino, already sweet beyond drinkable. He reached into his pocket, and he pulled out the lewdest Sheela na Gig he had been able to find in the museum gift shop. "Well, my dear, I lost Inga, and I'm about to lose Kara. At least I won't lose you."

Kara returned and saw the small figurine. "Larsson, I hope you have a sales receipt for that."

He laughed and put her back into his pocket, along with Kathleen's zeolite crystal. A loudspeaker announced his flight was ready to board.

"Time to go." Kara's usual sassy tone was missing.

She held his hand as they approached the security checkpoint.

"Both of you going?" asked the British Airways agent.

"Just me," Cal said, reaching for his ticket and passport.

Kara pulled him aside.

"I want to show you this." She handed him a small envelope. "My British Airways ticket for November 23. I'm coming for Thanksgiving dinner, provided you can find an extra seat at the table. It's nonrefundable, so I'm afraid you're stuck with me."

"We can always throw in one more potato." After a lingering embraced, Cal walked through the metal detector. He turned and blew her a kiss. "Good-bye, my love."

Kara mouthed her answer. *Good-bye, my love.*

Acknowledgments

Steel Wombs was born in 2005. The first draft was completed in four months. As I wrote, I was listening to a radio show. All I had to do was put on paper what I heard in my mind. After several revisions, it spent eight years in my closet until my wife, Betty, read it and urged me to finish the process by seeking outside comments. If it hadn't been for her encouragement, the manuscript would still be in the closet. Then I did something that is generally not recommended when getting a novel reviewed—have friends do it. The folks I asked were well read, insightful, and honest. Their comments and suggestions were invaluable. They pointed out many and glaring weaknesses and where the manuscript could be improved. It never would have gotten to this stage without them, and I thank them more than I can say. They are Judy Halesky, Paul Halesky, Ingrid Kelly, Byron "Dutch" Souder, and Marilyn Souder. Special thanks go to Nora Esthimer Gaskin, a published author and professional editor, living here in Chapel Hill. Her contributions were many, not the least of which included pointing out where I killed the action with unnecessary verbiage, and long sections that did nothing to move the story along, to say nothing of numerous detailed editorial corrections. Finally, I thank Lulu Publishing Services and its editorial staff, especially Joy E. for a careful and excellent review that greatly improved Steel Wombs. In the end, I take full credit for mistakes and missteps you may find.

About the Author

R. C. Lindholm taught geology at the George Washington University after earning a PhD at Johns Hopkins University. He now lives in North Carolina, south of Chapel Hill, with his wife, Betty, and cat, Slippurr.

Steel Wombs is his first book of fiction. Before retiring, he'd written numerous articles for professional geologic journals, as well as *A Practical Approach to Sedimentology* (Allen and Unwin, 1987). After retiring and moving to North Carolina, he wrote *Lindy's Identification Keys for Native Plants Growing in the North Carolina Triangle* (2002).